SEA CHANGE

SEA CHANGE
Peter Burchard

Farrar Straus Giroux
NEW YORK

For my children and grandchildren

SEA CHANGE

The Summerhouse

I

The night before that special day, Alice said good night to her parents and sister, left the comfort of the parlor, and began what sometimes seemed a fearsome journey to her room.

Until three years or so ago, a servant named Rosie, sensing her uneasiness, had often waited on the landing and walked with her to the back of the house. Even now, though Alice was too old to fear the dark, Rosie sometimes waited there. But Rosie had this evening off and Alice climbed the stairs alone, moving toward the picture on the wall above the landing. The painting, showing two bucks locked in deadly combat in a deep ravine, had always frightened Alice. Now, glancing at the terrible scene, she swung around a newel post and mounted the remaining steps.

The upstairs hall was not as dark as usual. Rosie must have lit the lamp in Alice's room before she went out. Alice had to pass three doors, all dark and partly open, before she reached the band of light. She made a sudden, headlong dash. Once in her room, she looked around. On the other side of her four-poster bed stood shelves containing her books, some of which she'd had since she was very young. On top of the shelves were rows of animals and dolls. Her favorite was Bear, who stared at her with shining eyes, as if to tell her to be brave, but there were shadows in her room and her heart was beating fast.

Alice knelt, flipped up her ruffled spread, and saw that nothing but a chamber pot was under her bed. As she pulled her nightgown over her head, hating the fleeting seconds of blindness, she heard footsteps on the stairs. Her mother was coming to kiss her good night.

Alice jumped into bed, pulling up the sheet and the light cotton blanket. As she lay, with her head on the pillow, her eyes were level with the doll's house Uncle Ted had given her six or seven years ago. Above it hung a picture from a fairy tale of a castle on an island where a princess lived alone.

Mother neither paused nor spoke but went straight to the window, raised the sash a couple of inches, then turned and smiled down at Alice. In the soft light of the lamp, her mother's face was beautiful. She wore simple diamond earrings and had about her an aroma of perfume.

Alice propped herself up on an elbow, forming words, speaking in a kind of whisper. Her mother hadn't heard a sound in years. She read lips but she had trouble understanding even members of her family. Her mother said, "I can't understand you. Come into the light."

6

Alice sat up, looked into her mother's eyes, and, emphatically moving her lips, formed the words "I love you, Mother."

Her mother bent, held Alice's shoulders, and kissed her cheek. "Dear child, I love you, too." She straightened up and, as she turned to leave the room, said good night. Although she knew her mother wouldn't hear, Alice called good night to her. Reluctantly, she raised the chimney of her lamp and blew out the flame.

At first, the night was very still. Then she heard a cricket's song. She heard the rustle of the trees she knew so well. As she drifted into sleep, something made her wake again. At first, the sounds were very faint, the notes of a waltz. They must be coming from the riverboat that passed her window every night on its way to Albany.

In her mind's eye, Alice saw the people dancing. She swung out of bed and stood at her window. Moonlight sparkled on the water. Soon the riverboat appeared, thumping steadily upstream, a red light gleaming near her bow. The music swelled and then grew faint again, weakened by a vagrant breeze. Alice saw herself aboard the boat with Uncle Ted, who wasn't young but was slim and very handsome. It was natural that she thought of him. He had promised to visit tomorrow, but even if he hadn't been coming to visit she would have thought of him when she heard the music and saw the boat, because she loved him very much. He had a boat of his own, and every spring, no matter what, following the schools of shad and the migratory birds, he sailed north from New York City. At night, he sat on the edge of her bed and told her stories. When, after staying several

7

days, he trimmed his sails and headed back toward New York City, Alice went to the summerhouse, high on a bluff, and watched until he disappeared.

2

In the morning Alice dressed and went downstairs. She moved through the pantry and into the kitchen. The room was large, with cabinets all around. A huge black stove stood against an inside wall, and a table and chopping block were in the middle of the room, surrounded by ladder-backed chairs and a couple of stools. Rosie, pink-cheeked, smiling, sat on one of the stools, wearing an apron, polishing silver. "My, but you're early."

"So are you, Rosie."

"Guests this weekend."

"When you finish the silver, I wonder if you'd tie a ribbon in my hair."

"You know I will. You've combed it nicely for a start."

"Let me help you with the silver."

"Mind you don't soil your pretty blue dress."

Alice put an apron on, sat down on the other stool, picked up a fork, and, using a brush, polished its tines. "Did you light my lamp last night?"

Rosie blushed. "I hope your father didn't mind."

"Why would he mind?"

"You know why."

Thinking of the bell that hung in the hall, remembering the coils of rope and pairs of gloves beside the win-

8

dows in the bedrooms, Alice nodded. "He once saw a village burned to the ground."

"Yes. In the war, when he and James were in their teens."

Rosie's husband, James, drove for them and kept the grounds. Long ago, he'd been in Father's regiment. Alice said, "Mother told me."

When they'd finished polishing the silver, Rosie said, "There's a setting for eight."

"I only count five, including Uncle Ted."

"Your sister Helen and her husband will be here. And your mother said to set a place for someone else."

Uncle Ted always sailed with strong young men, sometimes the sons of friends of his, but they lived aboard the boat and kept to themselves. Alice frowned and said, "A stranger." Then she laughed. "Tall and dark." She slid off the stool and glanced at the door. "I think I'll go walking."

Rosie looked at the clock. "Half an hour to breakfast," she said. "Shall I braid your hair?"

"No, thank you, Rosie. I just want a ribbon." Alice scrubbed and dried her hands while Rosie stood up and opened a cabinet. "Here. Yellow for spring." As she fluffed up the bow, she said, "My, but you're pretty."

"I'm not and you know it."

Rosie laughed. "I always tell the truth," she said.

Alice stood outside the door, like a cat about to venture forth. The river gleamed above its distant banks, which were green and blanketed by apple orchards. Sunlight scorched the morning mist. Two gulls, whose wings were almost touching one another, drifted high above the

9

water. Alice walked among her mother's flower beds, glancing at the carriage house where James and Rosie lived. She ran across a stretch of lawn, toward a giant copper beech. As she walked around the tree and approached the summerhouse, she slowed, stopped, and, catching her breath, began to walk.

Railroad tracks ran on both sides of the river. Across the way was a passenger stop. Far below the summerhouse, hidden by the banks and trees, freight trains traveled on this side, and in the fall, migrant workers, moving north to the vineyards, followed the tracks. At night they stopped, and now and then some of them walked up the hill and stood outside the kitchen door. Father never gave them money. He let Rosie give them food and once, when it was raining hard, he told a man who came alone that he could sleep in the summerhouse. By the following morning, the weather had cleared and Alice saw *six* migrant workers coming from the summerhouse, bedraggled, sleepy, moving toward the kitchen door. One was a dark and brooding man whom Alice feared. She felt violence in his stare, and one night soon after, he'd burst into her troubled dreams and she'd awakened, thrashing, screaming. Two years ago, a minister had set up living quarters for the men, and since then, Father had turned them all away. But Alice never quite forgot the brooding man and still approached the summerhouse with caution.

Now all she saw were a pair of swallows, tending a nest they'd built under the eaves. At first, they set up a terrible fuss, but when they saw she meant no harm, they settled down. Alice sat on the railing and studied the river. The wind was blowing straight upstream. She said aloud, "He'll be here soon."

She stared at the river twenty minutes or so, then turned and walked back. The house was white against a stand of spruce that screened it from the River Road. Its roof was wet with morning dew, and as it dried, it sent up a cloud of steam. As Alice moved across the lawn, starlings fluttered near a chimney.

Rosie called, "Your family's waiting. Go along."

The dining room was all dark wood, spotless linen, polished silver, and cut glass. Mother, Father, and sixteen-year-old sister, Florence, who was short and dark, sat at their places waiting for Alice. Mother smiled and Father said, "Good morning, Alice."

"Good morning, Father."

Father was tall and had a neatly trimmed beard. He said, "You're late."

"I'm sorry, Father. I was in the summerhouse."

Florence asked her, "Any sign of Uncle Ted?"

"No. Not yet."

Her mother asked Alice, "What did you and Florence say?"

When Alice, pointing and gesturing and moving her lips, repeated what they'd said, her mother nodded. Then she said emphatically, "After breakfast, James will drive me into town. Alice, I want you to come."

Most days, Alice liked to go to town; today she didn't want to go. She wanted to take up her vigil again. She had a vision, clear as life, of Uncle Ted walking up the sloping lawn, seeing her, waving wildly, running up and hugging her. He'd call her Peaches, as he always did.

Thinking of going to market with Mother, Alice made a face. Florence whispered, "Be careful."

3

James stood beside the open carriage. He had a long, pleasant face and bright blue eyes. His nose was pink. He wore a top hat only when Father insisted—when Alice's parents went out at night and when they went to church on Sundays. Now he wore a light tweed cap, which gave him the look of a country squire. Bending toward the metal step, making sure that Mother's foot was in its center, he helped her up and into the carriage. As Alice stepped in, he gave her a wink.

James took his seat and flicked the reins above the rumps of Nell and Dan. The carriage moved along the drive, through the gates, and turned into the River Road.

When they were still two blocks away from Anthony's Fruit and Vegetable Market, Alice could see the red and white canvas awning shining in the filtered sunlight. Main Street was alive with wagons, carriages, and horses. Shoppers gathered on the sidewalks, talking. As the carriage passed the bakery, Alice smelled cinnamon buns. James greeted the blacksmith and doffed his cap to Mr. Pierce, who owned the bank. Alice saw her classmate Betsy Clark with a friend, dodging shoppers, joking, smiling. Once in a while, James drove Alice to the house of a friend who lived in town. Then Alice had the kind of freedom Betsy had, but mostly Alice stayed at home.

In good weather, Tony put his produce under his awning, in barrels and bins. There were things from his hothouse, out-of-season vegetables, and fruit shipped up from Florida, lemons, oranges, and limes. James grew vegetables at home but they were often late, and in the spring, Mother went to Tony's often.

As soon as she stepped down from the carriage, Mother saw a crate of grapefruit, reached through the slats, and poked at one. Mother hated to ask about things because, when Tony talked to her, she never understood a word. Alice found Tony inside the store. He beamed at her and told her the price. "If you buy by the crate, I'll give you ten percent off. They won't spoil for two or three weeks."

Alice nodded, went back to her mother, and tried to tell her what Tony had said. Her mother frowned. "How much?" she asked.

Alice couldn't make her understand about the ten percent. Her lips grew tight. She tried again, to no avail. Mother said, "I forgot my pad and pencil. Maybe Tony—"

Alice went inside again. This time a man was talking to Tony. At first Alice listened, but the man talked altogether too much, *about nothing at all*. Alice said, "Excuse me, sir."

The man just frowned and kept on talking. He said the summer would be damp. He knew he'd suffer from arthritis. His wife had severe headaches; the doctor prescribed a treatment but it hadn't worked at all. Even Tony grew impatient. "What is it, Miss Alice?"

Alice said, "I can't make Mother understand."

Tony turned back to the man and explained. "Alice's mother is deaf," he said. He wrote a message on a pad,

13

tore it off, and gave it to Alice. As she turned, she heard the man say, "That's pathetic."

Alice faced the man and asked, "What's pathetic?"

"It's pathetic that your mother—"

"Mother's not at all pathetic. You're a *bore*." She spun around and walked away. Her lips were pale. Her hands were shaking. As Alice gave her the message, her mother asked, "What is it, child?"

Turning away, reaching into a barrel of apples, Alice picked one up and rubbed it against the back of her hand. It was green, with a pink blush near its stem. Her mother touched her arm and said, "I know it's hard for you sometimes when I can't understand."

Alice put the apple down and, turning back, gave her mother a sorrowful glance. Then, all at once, she went to her and hugged her tightly.

When they had finished shopping, James drove them back along Main Street and turned into the River Road. Alice's mother said, "Thank you for coming. I know you didn't want to."

Alice faced her mother and formed the words "I'm glad I came."

Her mother smiled. "I needed you." Then she said impatiently, "It was more than that today. Florence could have come with me. Today I—"

Alice waited.

"I wanted to talk to you before Uncle Ted—before he came. I know you're very fond of him."

Chin down, so her mother wouldn't see, Alice said, "I love him."

Unaware of what Alice had said, her mother went on.

"I should have told you when he wrote me. Ted is bringing someone with him. He's engaged."

Alice looked as if she'd been struck in the face. Pointing at herself, she said, "He said he'd marry me someday."

"You know he wasn't serious." She paused. "Ted's been engaged at least four times. He's forty-one. This time, I think he really means it."

Alice's voice was small and unsteady. "What's her name?"

"Adelaide."

"Adelaide's a silly name." She trembled and cried, "Now I can't love him anymore."

Her mother, missing everything she said, reached out and took her hand. Alice drew back. James, having overheard, hoping to distract her, teased, "You have me to love, Miss Alice."

Alice listened to the clicking sounds of horseshoes hitting random stones and to the steady creak of springs. Her voice rose slowly, surely, as she said, "I like you very much but I don't *love* you. Anyway, you're already married, James."

James said, "Now, about your Uncle Ted. You'll get over it in time."

Glancing at the sunlit elms that arched above the road, Alice said, "Damn Adelaide."

James turned, looked down, and frowned. "Don't say things you wouldn't say if your mother—"

"All right, James." Tears streaked her cheeks. As she dried her eyes she said, "I'll behave, but I have to tell you, James, that Adelaide will never, *ever* be a friend of mine."

When she was sad and out of sorts, a drive along the River Road almost always made Alice feel better. The horses' rumps moved rhythmically beyond the dashboard of the carriage. Sparrows rose ahead of them, wheeled, and settled in the ruts behind. A white moth fluttered in the underbrush. Still, Alice felt the awful weight of knowing Uncle Ted loved someone else, probably someone he'd only just met. She stared at her hands. James whistled softly to himself. Alice recognized the tune. "When Johnny Comes Marching Home." Why couldn't he forget the war? She tapped her foot. She *did* love James, though she'd never tell him so.

Back at the house, James drove to the carriage entrance. As he handed Mother down, he said, "Miss Alice, I'm sure you'll help me carry the groceries into the kitchen. I don't want to break the eggs."

"Yes, I will." She smiled.

"There. That's better. Miss Alice, it's wrong to blame your uncle for wanting to do what most men do, for wanting to marry, and you can't blame Miss Adelaide. She must love him as you do."

"That's impossible, James."

After James had left the kitchen, Rosie said, "You're upset. What's the trouble?"

"Nothing much. Mother told me—" As tears began to rise again, Alice said, "I'll tell you later."

"There now, child. Don't brood about it. Take a walk. Forget your troubles for a while."

Alice walked slowly, passing the carriage house, twisting her handkerchief, thinking, and hoping. Her hope became a certainty. Uncle Ted had always tired of his fiancées because he loved Alice. Surely Mother must be wrong. This time, he didn't really mean it at all. He'd tire of Adelaide as he had of the others. They'd probably already quarreled and she wouldn't be with him. Everything would be all right. She knew it would. She hurried to the summerhouse.

4

She hadn't been waiting for more than an hour when she saw three snow-white sails in the mist on the opposite shore. The bow of the boat pointed straight toward the bluff where the summerhouse stood.

A footbridge spanned the railroad tracks and wooden steps led down to the dock. Alice almost left the summerhouse, ran down the hill, and crossed the bridge, but something kept her where she was.

The boat was far below the summerhouse but Alice could see Uncle Ted at the helm. There were two or three other people on board. As Alice tried to sort them out, the schooner sailed behind a clump of pine. Frustrated, Alice stood on her toes. The boat had disappeared completely.

She stood near the copper beech, whose branches almost touched the ground. Its leaves were dark and menacing. Florence and Alice had once thought that the branches sheltered gnomes. Alice sat down on a rock beside the tree. From where she was, she could see the bridge but couldn't be seen from the house or the stable. She pulled her knees up to her chin.

SEA CHANGE

As she watched the ferry leave the opposite shore, she thought of the purser who let Alice and her sister ride all day for just five cents and sometimes took them to the wheelhouse. Last Christmas, Uncle Ted had come for a week. The river had been frozen solid and he'd had to hire a cutter to bring him across. Alice had watched as the train arrived and as the sleigh crossed the ice.

Now Uncle Ted appeared on the bridge. Someone was with him, a woman wearing a broad-brimmed hat and a light pink muslin dress. One of her hands was on the crown of her hat and the other was resting on Uncle Ted's arm. Behind them, a young man carried their bags. Alice gasped. She felt a tightness in her chest. The woman moved with self-assurance. She was probably pretty, but Alice didn't wait to see. She slid slowly off the rock and, putting the tree between herself and the couple, ran around to the front of the house. A horse and buggy stood by the door. Helen must be here. Alice groaned, ran up the steps, and entered the hall.

Hearing a buzz of talk in the parlor, she stood stock-still. She glanced at the landing, wanting to go upstairs and hide, but she knew that she was trapped.

Helen's voice rose high above her husband's laugh. "It's perfect nonsense. Alice will get over it."

Alice blushed. She crossed the hall and burst into the parlor. "Get over what?" she screamed at Helen.

Her sister had a haughty air. She raised her chin an inch or so. "Don't scream at me. We were talking privately."

Her husband, Jim, was short and wore a mustache. "Hello, Alice." He smiled. "You mustn't mind gossip."

"I do mind gossip."

"Come, come. We all love you."

"You show it in a funny way. I—"

Her father interrupted. "Someone's at the sun-porch door. It's probably Ted." As he left the room, he glanced at Alice, as if to tell her to calm down.

"Yes, Father," she said. She stood beside the chair where her mother was sitting. Her sister Florence said, "Alice, think of our guest. How would you like to be meeting six people you'd never, *ever* seen before and under—"

Out on the sun porch, Uncle Ted said, "Hello, Will. We've just barged in." He laughed. "Now that you have a telephone, I should have phoned you from West Point." In a strong, respectful voice, he said, "Will, this is Adelaide."

Alice watched the parlor door as the three of them came through. Awkward as he sometimes was, Father stood aside and said, "Ted, you make the introductions."

Adelaide's light pink dress was gathered tight around her waist. Her arms were slim. Her hands were long and beautiful.

Mother stood up. She said, "Welcome."

Uncle Ted beamed, gave Mother a hug, stood back, and looked around the room. His blue eyes twinkled as he said, "Here. Let me introduce you all." Adelaide was very gracious and her voice soft. When Uncle Ted presented her to Alice, his expression changed a little. He turned to Adelaide and said, "Peaches, come and meet my future wife."

Alice stared. Adelaide had dark brown eyes. She wasn't pretty in the least. Her mouth was large. The base of her nose was much too broad. Alice *hated* Adelaide, and

19

Adelaide made matters worse by behaving perfectly. She *didn't* say how much she'd looked forward to meeting dear Alice or how much she'd heard about her. She took a single step toward Alice, held out her hand, and said, "How do you do?"

A thin blue vein traced its course along the back of Adelaide's hand. Alice closed her eyes a moment, and when she opened them, she spoke. "I can't shake your hand," she said.

Adelaide's eyes widened slightly. She blinked and nodded. "I see," she said. "Maybe someday we'll shake hands."

"Never."

Father pushed past Uncle Ted, stepped in front of Adelaide, took Alice firmly by the wrist. Alice said harshly, "I'll go by myself. I *want* to go. Father, let me go upstairs alone."

Adelaide spoke to Father. "Please don't punish her," she said. "I think—I'm sure I understand."

Alice said, "No, you don't. You don't understand at all."

Father glanced at Adelaide. "I'm sorry," he said, steering Alice through the door. In the hall he glared at her. "You're just plain rude."

Alice raised her chin and said, "Father, please let go of me."

Her father's face was red. "No," he said.

As they moved up toward the landing, Alice glowered at the painting of the deer. Knowing it was Father's favorite, she said, "I wish you'd take that picture down. It's a truly hateful thing."

"Sometimes you're a hateful child."

In her room, Alice sat down on her bed and looked up at her father. He shook his head. "Two years ago I spanked you," he said. "Your mother made me promise never to spank you again. If I hadn't made that promise—"

"I suppose I deserve it." She pressed her lips together, hard.

"I think you do." He sat beside her, giving her an unexpected, tender look. "I'm mystified. I know you're fond of Uncle Ted but— You're twelve years old. Uncle Ted is almost forty."

"Uncle Ted is forty-one."

"Forty-one. You can't— You—" Father raised his hands in despair. "Why not give Adelaide a chance?"

"I won't give Adelaide a chance."

Father stood up abruptly. "You're a naughty, heartless child. What's the sense in talking to you?"

"No sense at all."

Father glared, turned around, and left the room. He shut the door. Alice frowned and stared at it. Her lower lip quivered; her eyes overflowed. As she cried into her pillow, she whispered in a muffled voice, "Everyone's against me now, except maybe James and Rosie."

5

Someone knocked. Alice sat up. "Who is it?" she asked.

A solemn voice said, "Uncle Ted."

Alice put aside the book she was reading. "Go away."

"Please, Peaches. Let's talk."

"Just a minute." Alice stood up and straightened her dress. She went to the washstand, wet a face cloth, and dabbed at her eyes. She pulled the ribbon off her hair, smoothed it out, and picked up her comb. Uncle Ted said, "Hurry up, Peaches."

Alice combed her hair, plumped up her pillows, sat against them, and called, "Come in."

Uncle Ted was holding a tray. In a joking voice he said, "My arms are tired."

"Why didn't you set down the tray?" Not waiting for an answer, she asked, "Can you tie a decent bow?"

He put the tray on Alice's table. "What a question. I can tie as good a bow as anyone. I'm a sailor. Sailors have to tie good knots."

"I never thought of a bow as a knot."

"It's a kind of knot," he said. "I'll tie one after you've finished your lunch."

As Alice started eating, she said, "You've cut up my meat."

"Rosie cut it. I'm only the butler."

Alice balanced the tray on her lap while Uncle Ted sat on the edge of the bed. As Alice ate, she studied him. He was handsomer than ever. His face was tan and at the corners of his eyes were thin white lines, crow's feet some people called them.

Uncle Ted knew when to be quiet and *how* to be quiet. He seemed always at his ease. At last he said, "You've changed since Christmas."

"Yes," she said. "I'm meaner now."

He laughed. "You've grown."

Trying to parrot him, she said, "My, how you've grown."

Uncle Ted said patiently, "I didn't see the change downstairs. I see it now. You're more mature."

"Not mature enough for you."

He gave her a thoughtful look before he said, "Peaches, you're my own true love."

Alice stabbed at a small piece of meat. She pushed a couple of peas aside. She wanted to speak, to tell him that she loved him, too, but she knew if she did she'd start to cry. She didn't want to cry again.

Uncle Ted settled down on the foot of the bed. "Sometimes life is very sad."

Alice thought of Uncle Ted as a man of the world. He knew a great many glamorous people down in New York. How could he think life was sad? With a touch of bitterness, she said, "Your life is never, *ever* sad." Uncle Ted got up and stood at the window. Alice added, "Women like you. Mother says you've had a lot of women in your life."

"Does she now." Uncle Ted said suddenly. "If I tell you something, will you promise not to talk about it?"

"I can keep a secret, Uncle Ted."

"No. It's not that it's a secret. Just don't mention it again, unless I do."

"All right."

"When I was young, I loved a woman very much. She loved me. We planned to marry. I made her a little mahogany box, inlaid with other kinds of wood. You saw it once, when you came to visit me."

"I remember. It was filled with treasures. I remember a locket, shaped like a heart. It had a diamond in its center."

He nodded. "Yes."

"It had a photograph of you inside. Anyway, I hope the woman liked the box. But why—"

"Before I finished it, she died."

Alice glanced at Uncle Ted. "Oh," she whispered.

"That was many years ago."

"It still hurts you?"

"Yes. It hurts to talk about it."

"Do you love Adelaide as much as the woman who died?"

He nodded. "Yes, I think I do."

"I've heard there are people who love only once."

He said sadly, "There are very few of those." As an afterthought, he added, "There are many kinds of love."

"Adelaide isn't pretty at all."

"She has a pure and loving heart."

"You can't expect me ever to like her."

"You're jealous of her. It will pass."

"Maybe."

"I hope it will." He stood up. "I haven't eaten my dessert. Rosie's saving two desserts."

"Can we eat them in the kitchen?"

"No. We'll eat them in the dining room."

"Please tie the ribbon in my hair."

6

Rosie had left two places set at the dining-room table, across from each other. Alice said, "I'll go ask Rosie for dessert."

"I missed my coffee. See if there's any left."

Alice came back and they both sat down. Alice asked, "Why is everything so quiet?"

"Your father had to go to town. One of his workers was injured this morning."

"Father doesn't make much noise. Where are the others?"

"Adelaide took your mother and Florence down to the dock to look at my boat."

"I hope Helen went home."

"Yes. They left right after lunch. What did Helen do to you?"

"I heard her talking to the others about—" She blushed. "She *laughs* at me sometimes."

Rosie brought two pieces of cake, a glass of milk, a coffeepot whose spout released a cloud of steam, and one of Mother's cups and saucers, blue with a band of gold around the rim. As she left the room, she glanced back at Alice and Alice said, "Thanks for sending up my lunch."

"You're welcome, Miss Alice."

When they had eaten their cake, Uncle Ted poured a second cup of coffee. He took a sip. Gently he said, "We're leaving tomorrow. We have a date in Garrison tomorrow night."

She swallowed hard. "Everything's changed. I *knew* it would. You won't come as often and won't stay as long."

"We may come oftener. Who knows? This time—"

"This time it's different."

"Yes, it is. I'll tell you why."

She touched the tip of her nose with her forefinger. "Please do."

He brought out a thin cigar. "Do you mind if I smoke?"

She nodded. "Yes, I hate the smell."

Uncle Ted laughed. "So does Adelaide." He put the cigar back into its case. "I started to tell you why we're leaving tomorrow. You know I love and respect your father, but he's shy and he has trouble putting visitors at ease." He looked down at his cup. "I talk to you too freely sometimes."

Alice was silent. At last she said, "I like the way you talk to me. I understand."

He nodded. "Adelaide can't talk to your mother, at least not yet. I knew this visit might be hard and so—"

Alice took a sudden breath. "When did you decide to leave tomorrow?"

He reached out and touched her hand. "Peaches, *you* didn't drive us away. We made our plans before we came."

They went through the sun porch and out to the lawn just as Adelaide, Mother, and Florence were crossing the bridge. Uncle Ted waved and Florence waved back. Alice moved forward and stood by a rock, where Mother had planted impatiens and pinks. Adelaide said, "Hello, Alice."

As Mother and Florence walked away with Uncle Ted, Alice looked straight into Adelaide's eyes. "Nobody told me to say this," she said.

Adelaide nodded. "Good," she said.

"I was rude to you. I'm sorry."

"I did worse things than that when I was young."

Alice wanted to know what she'd done but didn't want to ask. "Uncle Ted thinks I'm jealous."

"Maybe you are. Maybe both of us are."

"*You* jealous of *me?*"

Adelaide smiled. "You won a place in your Uncle Ted's heart long before he even *looked* at me."

"I don't suppose you've known him long."

"I met him many years ago. He scarcely noticed me back then."

Alice asked, "How old are you now?"

"I'm twenty-six. I first met your uncle when I was fourteen." She turned, as if to keep on walking. "Would you like to play a game?"

When grownups were at a loss, it seemed they always mentioned games. Alice asked, "What kind of game?"

"I was thinking of checkers or cards, but I suppose that, on a day like this, we should enjoy being outdoors."

Alice surprised herself by saying, "We have croquet. It's all set up."

"Let's ask Florence and Ted to play."

Alice didn't want to play croquet with Adelaide *and* Uncle Ted and Florence, too. She hesitated, but at last she said, "All right."

7

As they finished their third game, Adelaide said, "I'm tired." She confided in Alice. "Last night we stayed with friends in Duchess County. I woke up before dawn and lay in bed trying to imagine your house on the river and meeting you all. I couldn't go to sleep again."

"Then you'd better take a nap."

"I think I will." Adelaide and Uncle Ted had joked together while they were playing croquet. When they finished the game, Adelaide told him, "You were a beast to beat us so badly."

"I went straight for the wickets whenever I could." He winked. "I play a clean game."

After Adelaide went to her room, Father appeared. He and Uncle Ted started to talk. They lit cigars and wandered off.

As Alice put away the mallets and balls, she knew she *had* to be alone. Avoiding the sun porch, where Mother was sitting, she skirted the house, walked around the copper beech, and stood beside the summerhouse. This afternoon, the river was gray; in the center of the stream ran a swift and tortuous crease, a sign of a strong, unpredictable current.

Until four years or so ago, Alice and Florence had had a nurse, a woman always dressed in black, tall and forbidding, who had ruled them with a hand of iron, threatening them with fire and brimstone. She told them cautionary tales of children who had disobeyed their elders and drowned, been crushed to death by railroad trains, and fallen over rocky cliffs. Now, looking down, remembering those dreadful tales, Alice shivered and hugged herself. She thought of Uncle Ted at lunchtime, thoughtful, sad, standing at her bedroom window. Long ago, he'd told her how the river rose, at Lake Tear of the Clouds, how it ran down from the mountains, joined by other smaller streams, moved through a deep and silent gorge, before it flowed past New York City to the sea.

The sky above the Duchess County hills underwent a sudden change. First it was yellow, then it grew dark. Black clouds appeared. In the distance thunder sounded. If Uncle Ted hadn't been on the grounds, Alice might have run back to the house, but his presence made her brave. She stayed and watched the clouds build up, saw them rise and roll across the distant hills, pushed by a sudden northerly.

As the wind pulsed in the trees, Alice caught a glimpse of Uncle Ted running downhill toward the dock. Alice thought of chasing him but she guessed he'd send her back. The river grew black. Flecks of white appeared on its surface. The air was filled with dark red leaves. Alice stood on the summerhouse steps, smiling as she put her arms against her skirt to keep it down. It began to rain in almost horizontal sheets, wetting her skin and soaking her clothes. She stepped away from the summerhouse and moved across to the rim of the bluff. A strong gust blew her skirt against her legs. She had to fight to keep her feet and, stepping back, faced the wind, as if to defy it, laughing aloud because she didn't care how wet she was.

The rain let up. The sky was mottled and the grass was a brilliant green. Alice went to a place near the head of the bridge and looked down at the boat. Uncle Ted and two young men were talking together. They adjusted the lines. Uncle Ted noticed Alice, waved, stepped ashore, crossed the bridge, and gave her a hug. "Peaches," he said. His clothes were drenched. His hair was wild. He laughed and asked her, "What were you doing out in the storm?"

"When it came I didn't feel like going in."

He grinned. "I know exactly how you felt. I like to *sail* in storms sometimes." He took her hand, and talking happily, they walked together toward the house.

Everyone but Adelaide was sitting in the parlor having tea, and not thinking how they looked, Alice and Uncle Ted went in and greeted them. Right away, Mother said, "Where have you been?"

"I was in the summerhouse."

Father said, "Look at you. You've ruined your dress."

"It's not ruined. It's just wet."

He stood up. "Alice, don't talk back to me."

Uncle Ted said, "Come now, Will. Alice is high-spirited."

Alice nodded. "I was having an adventure."

Her father shook his head and said, "We all wondered where you were. Your mother worried when you didn't—"

"Father, it was *you* who worried."

Her father glowered. "That's enough. You'd better go upstairs and change."

8

Alice dried her hair and napped. She changed her clothes and spun around in front of her mirror, fluffing out her pale peach dress. Then she went downstairs. In the kitchen Rosie said, "You startled me!"

"Do you have a white ribbon?"

"Of course I do. White's just right." As she cut and tied the ribbon, Rosie said, "Try to last through supper, Miss Alice."

"Rosie, that's an awful thing to say."

"I know why you're out of sorts. It's only that—"

"James must have talked to you."

"James was only trying to help."

Alice nodded, bit her lip. "I'm sure he was. You and James are wonderful. You're my friends. I know sometimes I'm difficult, but I wish Father wouldn't tell me so and I wish Helen wouldn't be so high and mighty. Uncle Ted has been my friend since I was born. I—" She fought back tears.

"Try to think of something else."

"I have been trying. Just before I took a nap, I tried to think of Adelaide, of how she must have felt about the way I acted when I met her. Then I thought how good I'd feel to be her age and be engaged to Uncle Ted."

Rosie laughed. "I said think of *other* things."

Alice decided she'd had enough talk. She retreated to her room, looked into the mirror, and pinched her cheeks. She heard someone in the hall. Quietly she poked her head out. Adelaide was moving across to the head of the stairs. Evening sunlight filtered through a stained-glass window in the stairwell. In the warm glow, Adelaide was almost pretty. She paused a moment, looked up at the window, and then looked down, as if afraid to take a plunge. Slowly, feeling she'd intruded, Alice drew back into her room and stood quite still, waiting for the sound of footsteps on the treads.

31

SEA CHANGE

When Alice followed Adelaide, she found her family in the parlor. Father was holding a glass decanter bearing a silver necklace marked SHERRY. He passed the sherry to his guests and to Mother and then filled two glasses with grape juice. As he passed the juice to Florence and Alice, he said, "Here, girls. It won't be long before Florence can join us."

Florence said, "I don't much like the taste of sherry."

Alice winked at Uncle Ted. "I think it's *delicious*."

"You'll have to wait," Father said. "It's shocking how French children drink strong wines. It's no wonder the French are addicted to alcohol." He poured himself a glass of sherry.

Uncle Ted said, "There are stronger things than wine."

"Not in this house. Strong liquor is abhorrent." Father lowered his voice. "Sometimes James goes into town and drinks with friends. Last week he came home quite drunk. I told him, if he goes on drinking, I'll ask him to leave us."

Alice said, "Oh, Father, no!"

"It's entirely up to James." Having dismissed the subject, Father spoke to Adelaide. "Ted tells us you teach."

"Yes," she said. "I love my teaching."

"He says you teach art."

"Yes. Drawing and painting."

"What do you think of the things on our walls?"

Adelaide glanced at a very large portrait of a woman in black, whose hair was dark and parted in the middle. The woman wore a starched white collar. Her face was pale. Her lips were thin.

Adelaide looked down at the carpet. "My taste in art is strange," she said. "I think perhaps—"

Deliberately provocative, Alice said, "Father likes the painting on the wall above the landing."

Father frowned. "Don't interrupt."

Adelaide looked straight at Alice, then at Father. She said sadly, "Maybe we should change the subject. My opinions may divide us at the start of what I'd hoped might be a long and happy friendship."

Father grew a little huffy. "Surely you can see the merit in the painting Alice mentioned."

"Yes, I can. The artist was extremely skillful. The picture is strong and very dramatic, but its subject is repellent."

Alice took a quick, deep breath. Father bridled.

Uncle Ted spoke to Father. "Adelaide's taste in art may be strange but I'm glad she speaks her mind. I wish we all did that more often."

Adelaide said, "Thank you, Ted, but it was weak of me to say my taste in art is strange. It isn't strange. It's simply *mine*."

Adelaide's statement was followed by silence. Alice looked around the room. Mother, aware that something unpleasant had happened but not knowing what it was, expressed her sense of isolation. "Dear me," she said.

Father sat up straight and made no comment. Adelaide's lower lip twitched, just once. Alice, knowing she had stirred things up, said, "Everyone is much too quiet. Why don't we—"

Florence spoke up. "Hush," she said.

Alice glanced at Adelaide and, speaking to her father, said, "Her taste is *hers*. Why should that be so distressing?"

Uncle Ted said, "It shouldn't be. Still—"

Rosie stood in the doorway and announced, "Supper is served."

9

Uncle Ted, with a little help from Alice, kept the conversation going over soup. Adelaide, trying to draw Father out, said, "Ted tells me you were in the Civil War."

"In a New York regiment."

"You were young when you enlisted."

"Yes. I was a drummer boy."

"Ted says you were just sixteen. It's incredible to me that boys that age—"

Father interrupted her. "I seldom talk about the war."

Giving up, Adelaide turned to Mother. "The consommé is very good. I hope you'll compliment your cook."

Alice sat on Mother's left and, as she always did, translated things. She kept her statements short and simple. Adelaide, on Mother's right, watched Alice and, at last, said a word or two to Mother. Mother smiled. Uncle Ted, sitting next to Adelaide, said, "Good. You're learning fast."

Supper was a hearty meal. Father carved the roast of lamb and served the slices with potatoes sprinkled liberally with parsley. Rosie passed the peas and onions. More trouble started just before dessert. Father mentioned politics. He was a staunch Republican and Uncle Ted a Democrat. Adelaide talked to Florence, who hadn't said a word since soup, and Mother, seeing that everyone was busy talking, leaned toward Alice. Almost whispering, she asked, "What made your father cross when we were sitting in the parlor?"

"I can't talk about it now."

"Please try to tell me what it was."

Moving her lips and making no sound, Alice explained that they'd talked about art and Mother said, "Art?"

Alice nodded. Mother said, "How could that make Father cross?"

Adelaide overheard. "Tell her if you want to, Alice."

Alice wondered how to start. "Adelaide teaches school. She teaches art."

Mother nodded. "Yes, I know." She saw that Adelaide was listening and asked her directly, "How old are your students?"

Adelaide signaled six and then fourteen. She turned back to Florence and apologized for breaking off their conversation, and Mother, speaking only to Alice, asked, "Why did art make Father cross?"

Alice hoped her father hadn't heard the question. She grew tense. She tried to say that *she* had raised the subject of the painting of the deer, that Father had asked for Adelaide's comment, and when Adelaide had spoken honestly, Father's feelings had been hurt. The message was too complicated. Mother only shook her head. Alice felt cornered. She said, "Let me tell you later."

Mother shook her head again and said, "Please tell me."

35

Alice saw she couldn't leave things as they stood. She thought of asking Father to excuse her so she could get a pad and pencil, but if she did, Father would become involved. She clenched her teeth and shut her eyes.

Rosie brought in cherry cobbler, Alice's favorite dessert, but Alice scarcely noticed it. Mother, who was busy serving, didn't see how Alice felt and told her absentmindedly, "Try once more. Then if—"

"Please, Mother, I can't. Don't make me go on. I can't. I *can't*." She brought her fist down on the table, upsetting Mother's sherry glass.

As the stain spread, Father stood up. He glowered, first at the stain, then at Alice. "Go to your room."

Adelaide pushed her chair back. "No. Please don't send her to her room. In this case, she's not to blame."

Father said, "I'm sure I don't know what you mean."

"Just now she did her best to tell her mother what I said that upset you. Her mother failed to understand. When Alice saw that it was hopeless and her mother asked her to try again, she lost patience."

Father looked around, touched the watch chain on his vest, settled back, and stared at Adelaide as if she were a Chinese puzzle. "After what she said to you when you arrived, I'm surprised to see you looking for excuses for the child."

Adelaide stared back at him. "It must be hard for you to understand my tolerance. It's just that—I don't know." Adelaide's eyes filled with tears. "I *want* to understand her. Can't you see? Try to think how you might feel if every day—" She paused. "There are times when Alice simply *can't* convey these conversations. I must say a thing like that would drive me wild."

Father said, "There's no excuse for bad behavior in a child. Do you believe in discipline?"

"Of course I do, but"—she paused, and when she spoke again, she spoke quite fast—"I remember how I felt when I was Alice's age. It's a cruel time for girls."

Father's face grew very pale. He turned to Alice. "You can stay with us tonight, but in the future, if you lose your temper, I won't be so lenient."

After dessert, he rose abruptly from his chair. "Ted and I will go outside. None of you likes the smell of cigars."

10

When it was time for Alice to go to bed, everyone was in the parlor. Knowing that tonight Uncle Ted would tuck her in, Father and Mother kissed her good night. Father smiled. "Good night, child."

Adelaide said, "See you in the morning, Alice."

Florence, sitting in a corner reading, winked at Alice as she said good night to her. Alice was surprised and pleased to see Rosie sitting on the landing. Staring up at the painting, Alice reached for Rosie's hand. "I'm not afraid. I'll go alone." She laughed. "The journey isn't very long." Without the slightest hesitation, Alice went up. She undressed fast, put on her nightgown, washed her face, and combed her hair. Standing at her bedroom window, she looked down at the lawn. Streaks of light, from the kitchen, dining room, and parlor, weakened as they fanned out and disappeared into a great well of darkness near the bridge. The thunderstorm had cleared the air but, even so, the river and the sky were one. The lights along the distant shore hung as if suspended in a void.

Above the hush, she heard James, in the rooms above the carriage house, strumming his guitar and singing. She wished Father hadn't said he'd let James go if James didn't mend his ways, but she knew that Father wouldn't *ever* let James go, because they'd fought together in the war and everyone liked Rosie's cooking.

Alice sat against her pillows. She heard the sound of Rosie's voice rising above the clatter of dishes.

Someone came upstairs. "Hello, Peaches. You in bed?"

"Yes, Uncle Ted."

As he came in, he looked around the room and nodded. "People's rooms give them away."

"What does my room say to you?"

"A lot of things. Mostly that you're warm and loving. The doll's house brings back happy memories. I remember watching your hands as you arranged the furniture. You had an especially delicate touch."

"Did I really?"

"Yes, you did, and you still do." Glancing at her shelves, he said, "You're loyal to Bear."

"Mother sewed him up for me."

"It's hard to believe that in a year or so you'll put your dolls and animals away in the attic."

"Maybe I won't."

Uncle Ted took a deep and silent breath. "Peaches?"

"Yes."

He reached for something in one of his pockets. "I've brought you a present." He took out a tiny box, wrapped

38

in white and tied with a ribbon the color of the dress she'd worn at supper.

"I'd forgotten you bring presents."

Alice stared down at the package. She touched the bow. At last, she pulled the ribbon off. She unfolded the paper and opened the box. There, resting on a square of cotton, lay the locket, shaped like a heart, with a diamond in its center. Alice breathed, "Oh, Uncle Ted." She paused, then asked him, "Was it hers?"

His voice was soft. "Yes, it was. I gave it to her."

"I'll never tell a living soul."

He smiled. "Someday you'll want to tell *someone*, but don't forget you promised not to mention her unless I do."

"I never will. Does—does Adelaide mind—I mean that you loved someone else?"

"No, I'm sure she doesn't mind."

Alice slid her fingernail between the two halves of the locket and pried it open. Inside was the photograph. Alice said, "You're handsomer than you were then." She shut the locket. "Uncle Ted?"

"What's your pleasure?"

"Ask Adelaide to say good night to me."

He grinned. "I will."

After Uncle Ted had left, Alice put the locket away in a drawer. When Adelaide came upstairs, she stood in the hall and said, "May I come in?"

"Yes," Alice said. "Sit on my bed."

Adelaide sat up straight. "It's been quite a day," she said.

Alice nodded. "You and I are troublemakers."

"Goodness, I suppose we are. One has to stir things

up sometimes." Her hands clasped loosely in her lap, Adelaide relaxed a little. Her lips were moist. Her eyes were dark. Alice turned her covers back and went to Adelaide and hugged her. Then she sat down. Her feet swung just above the floor. "Will my parents ever understand me, do you think?"

Adelaide laughed. "If you help them. Don't you think they're making progress?"

"I suppose so."

"I told your mother I'd write her a letter tonight, about what happened in the parlor and at supper."

"Good. Mother likes letters."

"I hope she likes mine." Adelaide stood up and said, "Good night, dear child."

"Last night, my mother called me that: 'dear child.' I'm not a child."

"You're right. You're not." She laughed and, as a kind of afterthought, said, "Let's keep on being troublemakers."

"All right. Let's."

Sea Change

I

The cottage stood above the sea. A salt pond lay at the foot of the hill and, across its placid waters, came the sound of surf and sand.

Anne was fourteen and she liked to be outdoors, to walk and swim. When the summer sun was bright she seldom thought about the war. In the evening, when the air was faintly chilly, when the sky was filled with stars and she was inside the house, the enemy seemed very close.

This evening, as the sky turned pink, Anne and her mother sat together on the porch and faced the pond, the dunes, the sea. Anne's mother wore a light blue chambray shirt that matched her eyes. Though she moved and spoke with spirit, there was worry in her face. "Look there," she said.

Anne followed her gaze, and on the horizon she saw silhouettes of ships, all steaming east. "Three. No, four."

Her mother said, "I see at least six. There must be

more. They must be coming from New York. I'd have thought they'd have left after dark."

Anne's eyes were brown, her father's eyes. As she counted ships, she frowned. "I miss Daddy very much."

"We'll see him soon."

"I want him to be here *now*." Anne imagined his small ship, dwarfed by the North Atlantic seas. Last winter, he had sailed to the top of the world, north of Norway, Sweden, and Finland, to Murmansk, in the Soviet Union. The sea up there was filled with ice, and if his ship had been torpedoed, he would almost certainly have died.

Anne's mother stood up abruptly, touched the railing, scanned the sea. "Summer's coming to an end. I'd like to stay here through the winter, wouldn't you?"

"No. This place is much too lonely. We don't even have a *phone*. I'd miss my friends."

"I might miss mine. Still, I'd like to try it, once at least."

"We'd have to huddle by the fire. The water pipes would freeze and burst."

Her mother laughed. "My, how practical you are."

Shortly after it grew dark, they went inside. They moved around the house together, pulling down the window shades. They unrolled the blackout curtains and, at last, turned on some lights.

The house, though small, was comfortable. All the rooms were on one floor, their walls unfinished, the studs and stringers brown with age. Above the bedrooms was a loft, where Anne slept when they had guests.

The kitchen was a pleasant room. Its windows overlooked a turnaround and a pair of parallel dirt tracks leading to a county road that ran along the ridge. The kitchen table, circular and ringed with ladder-backed chairs, was covered with a checkered cloth and had a candle at its center, in a dish.

It was late and Anne was hungry. They were having flounder, new potatoes, salad, and a light dessert. In New York, they seldom ate seafood, but here, where it was fresh, they had it several times a week. Every morning, Anne's friend Jake DeBragga fished the ponds and estuaries near Menemsha in his dory, and at noon today, when she had bicycled to the post office, she had met him on his pier and watched him clean his catch. He had given her a pound or so of what he called yellowtails. "Take these," he'd said. "I don't charge my friends for fish."

Now, while her mother dipped the fish in melted butter and bread crumbs, Anne pulled down the oven door and, using a long kitchen fork, punctured one of the potatoes. "Done," she said. She washed and dried the salad greens and sliced tomatoes, while her mother lit the broiler and put in the yellowtails. Anne said, "Company tomorrow night. Are we having something special?"

"I haven't thought about it yet." She stared blankly into space, smiling faintly. Then she said, "I love Ted and Adelaide."

"So do I."

"Maybe we can buy some lobsters." As they sat down, Anne's mother smiled again. "This place will never lose its charm for me. It reminds me of what Daddy calls the good, gone days."

Anne knew that, twenty years or so ago, her mother and father had come quite often to this cottage. She knew that they had given parties here. In a corner of the living room stood an ancient phonograph, and beside it, in a cabinet, there were stacks of records. Once, Anne had listened to a few of them. They were scratchy and the voices seemed to her echoes of a carefree past. She asked her mother, "Was it the war that made things change?"

Her mother struck a wooden match and lit a candle. She said firmly, "Nothing ever stays the same."

"A lot of people wish things would."

"I don't. I'd die without the fun of change." Suddenly, as if she couldn't measure up to what she'd said, tears filled her eyes. "I hate this war. The men go off and play their deadly games while we sit here—" She stopped abruptly.

Anne said sharply, "Daddy *had* to go to war. You've told me that a thousand times."

Her mother nodded sadly. "Yes." Every night, before they ate, she closed her eyes, bowed her head, and said, "We thank you for this food."

Tonight Anne added softly, "Please bring Daddy back to us."

When they finished, Anne cleared off the table, while her mother served dessert. That morning they had ranged across the nearby hills and picked two quarts of blueberries. As they picked, they ate some of them, but there were plenty left, and they had a pint of cream from Beardsley's farm. They were silent as they ate.

Anne poked the berries remaining in the bottom of her bowl. This afternoon, when she had come back from Menemsha, she had brought a letter to her mother from her father. When her mother had seen it, she had given a cry and gone to her room, to read it alone. Anne knew how private letters were, but as she scooped up the last of her berries, she asked, "Can you—Will you read me Daddy's letter?"

Her mother reached across the table, took her daughter's hand, and squeezed. "Let's go outside. When we come back, I'll read you part of Daddy's letter."

As she pulled her hand away, Anne nodded. "Sure. Let's row across the pond and walk. We'll sleep much better if we do."

"I'll stack the dishes in the sink. We can wash them in the morning."

2

Anne shipped the oars, took off her sandals, and stepped into the shallow water. "Stay in the boat. I'll pull you in."

Anne's mother took her sneakers off and put them on the seat beside her. She was just about to stand when Anne gave the boat a tug. As Anne's mother sat down hard, she laughed. "Take it easy."

They took a path that led across the dunes and paused beside a clump of grass. As they watched a smudge of clouds move slowly east, the moon appeared, lopsided, blurred. Its reflection traced a path of shattered gold from the invisible horizon to the regiments of waves that swept the shallows, broke, and hissed across the sand.

In the unexpected light, Anne saw her mother start to speak, then shake her head before she said, "Sometimes I think about the German sailors lurking just offshore.

I fear U-boats for Daddy's sake. I'd like to see them *all* destroyed. Even so, if a German came ashore, I'd like to meet him face to face and talk to him. I think it might be comforting. After all, they're only men."

"If a German came ashore, he'd be afraid."

Anne's mother pushed away a strand of hair. She shuddered. "It won't happen. After all, when we destroy a submarine, its crew stands very little chance of ever seeing the light of day again."

"Let's go," Anne said. They walked together, to the wet sand, just above the waves, breathing in the salty air. Anne's mother, answering a sudden yearning, startled Anne by breaking loose and running toward a distant cliff. Anne followed her, caught up, and bumped against her playfully.

As her mother fell, she laughed. "No respect."

Anne said, "We joke more when Daddy's here. Why don't we clown around more often?" Anne took her mother by the hand, pulled her up, and tugged her toward the cliff. "Let's keep on walking. Gotta walk."

"I can't wait until tomorrow, to see Ted and Adelaide."

"What time do you think they'll come?"

"If all goes well, they should be here by one o'clock." She glanced at Anne. "You must be tired of constant adult company. Maybe, when the war is over, you can have good times down here, with people your own age."

"Sure, when peace comes and everyone can travel easily, I'll round up my New York friends and bring them here. Then, at night, we'll build a fire and cook hot dogs."

"You *are* deprived. Why not have a big clambake, with steamers, mussels, corn, and lobsters?"

"And cake and ice cream for dessert."

"Sure. Why not."

"How old were you when you had picnics on the beach?"

"I was sixteen. When I was fifteen, Father's business failed. Right after that, my parents sold the house upstate and moved to an apartment in New York. We came here to escape the heat. We took a house near Edgartown, a run-down little place."

"I know the house. You showed it to me last year."

"So I did. It's in a grove of stunted trees." Anne's mother puffed. "Slow down," she said. "I remember Father's face when he saw the furniture. Poor man. His pride was hurt."

"Was Aunt Florence with you then?"

"Florence was already married. I'd become an only child."

"Like me."

"Like you."

They walked until, ahead of them, a vast expanse of sand ended in a scattering of rocks below the cliff. The promontory, topped with grass and beach-plum bushes, rose above them, like a wave about to break. Anne had climbed it many times, but now, at night, it seemed much higher. As she stood and stared at it, a man appeared against the sky. Anne caught her breath. Jake had said that he sometimes walked across the hills at night. It must be Jake. She cupped her hands and shouted, "Jake, that you?"

The man stood still. Anne's mother turned and called, "Hello!" Still, he didn't say a word. Anne's mother whispered, "That's not Jake." She took Anne's hand and started moving, pulling her, then letting go. Together

51

they ran back to where they'd started walking. When they turned, they saw no sign that anyone was following. Anne giggled and her mother made a loud, explosive sound. Anne sucked in a sudden breath and laughed so long and hard she had to sit down on the sand. As she wiped away a tear, she said, "Now we're not so serious."

"I wonder why we're both so jumpy. We behaved like perfect fools."

They crossed the pond, tied up the boat, and padded up the sandy path that led to the cottage. They had left a lamp on in the kitchen but their blackout was almost complete. In back, they could see only a crack of light underneath the kitchen door. As Anne opened the door, the light was reflected in the chrome on their Ford convertible, which was parked canted over on a mound of grassy turf.

Inside, Anne's mother said, "I'll go get the letter now."

Anne sat at the kitchen table. Her mother came back and sat down across from her. "Daddy wrote this in July." She put her glasses on and read: "Last month, we encountered trouble in the Barents Sea but, though our ship was badly crippled, made it back as far as England, where our men enjoyed their liberty and Captain Tripp and I caught up on paperwork and watched, like mother hens, as welders crawled around our ship and sent up sparks. I went to London, for two days, to look up friends whose names you won't have any trouble guessing." Anne's mother paused. "He must mean Cousin John. He's stationed there. I can't think who the others are."

Not caring who the others were, Anne said, "Go on."

Her mother held the letter back a little, squinting as she read again. "We don't know where the fates will take us, and if we did, I couldn't tell you anyway. Awhile ago, I suffered terrible frustration when we docked at Brooklyn Navy yard and spent an hour at a pier, taking on supplies and fuel, before we had to leave again. I called you twice and I called Ted and Adelaide. No luck at all. It was torture, pure and simple. Maybe you'd gone to a movie that night. In any case, please don't stay home on my account. We almost always have a day in port and sometimes more."

As her mother turned the page, Anne could see her father's suntanned face, his downward-curving nose, his smile. Her mother said, "There's more. I hope to be in Boston or New York some time this summer, maybe for a week or so, so I can spend some time with you, in our cottage by the sea. I long to hug and kiss you both. When I—" Anne's mother glanced at Anne. "I'll skip this part and read the end."

Anne nodded. "Okay, Mom."

"Good night, dear ones. I love you both with all my heart." She got up suddenly and said, "I think I'll do the dishes now. You go ahead and read your book."

In bed that night, Anne lay awake and listened to the whisper of the grass outside her window and the pounding of the sea. The last line of her father's letter echoed in her memory. He'd spent ten days at home in April, when, following a sunny spell, the fruit trees by the reservoir had been in bloom. One day he had picked her up at school. She had come out with several friends and seen him pacing with the kind of energy that sometimes made him seem impatient. When he had seen her, he had grinned and done a pirouette. She'd laughed and told a friend of hers, "That's my dad."

The two of them had walked in Central Park and sat together on a terrace by the lake. She'd noticed that his dark blue uniform was out of press and crusted, here and there, with salt. She'd touched the gold braid on his sleeve. "Look. Your stripes are getting green."

He'd smiled at her and said, "The tarnish shows I really go to sea."

"Don't all sailors go to sea?"

"No. Some of them grow fat and soft in offices."

"You're my sailing hero, Dad."

The night he had left, he had tucked her in, held her hand, talked to her. Because his eyes were soft and brown, she had never been afraid to meet his gaze. He hugged her tightly and kissed her neck. She smelled the faint aroma of his shaving lotion on his skin and rubbed her hand across his cheek. He said, "I have to sail tonight."

"I know, Daddy."

Now, in the cottage by the sea, Anne closed her eyes and, for the second time that day, said, "Please bring Daddy back to us."

3

Next morning, wearing sandals and a bathing suit, with a towel draped around her shoulders, Anne moved through the living room. Her mother said, "Be careful when you cross the pond and please don't swim unless there's some-one swimming with you."

Impatiently Anne said, "Yes, Mom." A book lay on a table near the door. Anne picked it up. "Why don't you come?"

"Because I want to wash my hair."

Anne knew she'd rather go alone, but something made her say, "I'll wait for you to wash your hair. You can dry it on the beach."

"I'm much too vain."

The bottom of the screen door stuck. Anne kicked it. As she moved out to the porch, she squinted hard against the glare. She rowed across the pond and beached the boat between two others. As she started toward the dunes, a red ball rose against the sky and disappeared. She supposed that Gary Mackintosh would be there. He always was. He'd pester her until she swam with him and then he'd give her long and soulful looks.

Sure enough, he was there. It was Gary's beachball she had seen. He was playing with it alone. As he threw it up again, he saw her and let it fall and roll away. Trying to look dignified, he walked stiffly toward her. When he spoke, his voice went up, from baritone to tenor. "Hi," he said. He cleared his throat. "Where's your mother?"

"At the house."

"What a day. Look at the surf."

His conversation made her think of readers she had had in school when she was six years old. His skin was pink, his nose red. He stood in front of her and, with his big toe, drew a line across the sand. Anne worked hard to keep from laughing. She supposed she'd have to sit with him, at least until they'd had their swim. They moved toward his towel, which was spread out near his mother, who was lying on her stomach, dozing. Hearing somebody approach, she raised an eyelid, rolled an eye. "Good morning, Anne."

"Good morning, Mrs. Mackintosh."

Gary snatched up his towel. He retreated, beckoning. Anne nodded. Now, at least, they wouldn't have to listen to his mother, who delivered monologues about her fancy friends in Boston and New York, and complained about the rationing of gasoline. Anne put her towel down ten feet or so from several strangers, people in their early twenties. Gary followed, settled down. Glancing at her book, he said, *"Daisy Miller.* Do you like it?"

"Yes. So far."

"It's beautiful."

"I didn't think boys read such things."

"I finished it at school one night, in study hall. It made me cry. I had to kind of hide my face."

Anne glanced at him, turned away, and faced the sea. "I knew the ending would be sad. Don't tell me any more, okay?"

"Okay."

She scooped up sand and let it trickle through her fingers. "Any news about your father?"

"Two weeks or so ago we got six letters, all at once. One for me and five for Mom. He writes Mom an awful lot."

"She's lucky."

"Yes, she is. I wish she'd write him oftener."

"Don't you write him?"

"Sure I do. It's not the same."

Anne sat up and clutched her knees. She thought of mentioning her father, but instead, she jumped up and said, "Let's swim." She ran straight toward a cresting comber. Gary followed and they splashed ahead together. As they caught the full force of the wave, Anne staggered, spun around, and almost sprawled. She screamed and, grinning, rushed straight at the second wave, diving at its emerald curl, piercing it, then standing up to face a third.

The undertow was very strong but they found that they could go out fifty yards or so before the sand began to shelve. Anne let several small waves pass. She picked a big one, jumped up as it drew abreast of her, arched her body, floated, gathered speed, and planed. Arms pointing toward the burning sand ahead of her, she put her head down, held her breath, and let herself be carried in, until the power of the wave was spent.

Gary rode in on another wave. They swam until Anne's legs began to ache. She walked back to her towel, dried herself, and, tingling, stood a moment in the sun. Gary ran along the beach. When he came back, he caught his breath and said, "A day like this is worth a thousand winter days."

Put off by his enthusiasm, Anne said, "I dunno. I kind of like to skate and ski."

Gary said, "I—I do, too. I only meant—"

Anne softened. "You're right. It *is* a perfect day."

As they sat down, he said, "There must have been a storm at sea. It's strange to think that distant storms can make the waves build up like this." Suddenly, as if he thought he might have said a boring thing, he began to pat the sand. He glanced at her but didn't speak.

Anne said quickly, "Last night Mom and I came over here and walked awhile. We—"

"Go on," he said.

"It's hard to explain. There's not much chance that

German sailors will appear, not here at any rate, but last night Mom and I saw someone standing on the cliff and we absolutely panicked."

"You thought you saw a stranded German."

"Maybe, for a moment. I don't know. Not long before, Mom had said she almost wished that she could meet a German sailor face to face, but when we saw that man up there, she knew she didn't really mean it." Anne paused a moment, then went on. "I suppose that soldiers in the infantry have to *hate* the men they kill, but Dad doesn't feel that way at all. He says a bond unites the sailors of the world, that they all have to fight the sea."

"Still, they have to kill each other. I heard about a German submarine commander who machine-gunned sailors on a raft."

"I heard about that, too, but Dad knows someone who was *rescued* by a German submarine commander. Anyway, Mom and I sometimes talk about the Enemy, with a capital E. We don't mean the German armies or their fleet of submarines. For us, the Enemy is fear."

"My father thinks that, more than death, we fear a loss of dignity. Men who face a firing squad almost always stand up straight. Some even curse the riflemen." Sounding edgy, Gary said, "I fear the Japanese and Germans." He was silent, then said fiercely, "Look what they've done to us."

"I wonder when the war will end."

"Dad says it may go on for years. If it goes on long enough, *I'll* have to fight."

"Do you want to?"

"I don't know." Gary frowned.

Anne raised her chin and nodded shortly. Picking up a

broken seashell, brushing off the grains of sand that clung to it, she said, "It's good to talk to you."

4

Anne's mother sat behind the wheel. When she contemplated driving, she took on a puzzled look. The gearshift lever and the pedals might have been components of an instrument designed to baffle and disgrace a woman born when cars were very scarce and exploded when they started. She said, "The car's an oven, isn't it?" She turned the key, pulled out the choke, and, as if she were squashing an unwelcome bug, pressed her foot down on the starter button. When the car wouldn't start, she groaned and said, "No. Not again."

Anne said, "Push the choke back in."

"We could have walked but Uncle Ted is in his seventies and Adelaide is nearly sixty. Anyway, we'll use very little gas." Again she pressed the starter button; this time the engine racketed and died. The next time she tried, it started, coughed, and kept on running. Anne's mother shifted into first, released the handbrake, and engaged the clutch. Like a horse with one leg shorter than the other three, the car leaped forward, jerking, rocking, passed a clump of juniper, and, tracking nicely, crossed the field and climbed up to the county road. They headed west. Out at sea, a Coast Guard cutter on patrol cruised serenely, trailing an attenuated plume of white.

They swung around an isolated church, headed north,

then west again, going down a gentle slope. Four years earlier, Menemsha had been devastated by a hurricane. Now it consisted of fishermen's shacks, a Coast Guard station, and a building owned by Jake DeBragga and his wife, which contained a post office and a general store. In the harbor, moored and docked at flimsy piers, were lobster boats. Two draggers occupied a larger pier.

They stopped in a dusty parking lot in front of the DeBraggas' place. As they stepped down from the car, Anne's mother said impatiently, "Let's go see if they're in sight."

Anne thought she might collect the mail first, but instead, she joined her mother as she walked around the harbor, toward a hill. Standing on a gentle bluff, they looked out across the sound. Against a line of distant coast, they saw a pair of sails, a single hull, moving toward a buoy several hundred yards from where they stood. Anne's mother touched a locket hanging on a thin gold chain around her neck. "Long ago, they had a schooner. Now they have a little sloop. That must be it." She sat down on a patch of grass. She seemed a thousand miles away. Reaching out to bring her back, Anne said, "I see you wore your locket, Mom."

Her mother looked up, smiling. "Yes. I don't wear it every day because the chain is delicate. I'm afraid of losing it."

"I know it means a lot to you."

Staring at the distant sails, Anne's mother said, "It's wonderful how Uncle Ted has stayed lean and strong these many years."

"I guess he's led a healthy life."

"He was wild until he married Adelaide. Adelaide's

been good for him." As Anne sat down, her mother asked, "Who was on the beach this morning?"

"Mrs. Mackintosh and Gary and some people I don't know."

"I like Gary."

"He's okay. He's kind of *young*."

"He's exactly your age, Anne. I hope you were nice to him. He's as shy as he can be."

"I was very nice to Gary, Mom." She laughed again. "I was nicer than I've ever been to *any* boy."

"Good. I'm glad." She turned again, to watch the boat.

Anne said, "Let's go down and get the mail. By the time we come back up, they'll be close enough so they can see us."

"You go along. I'll wait here."

The post office consisted of a counter facing a display of magazines. Behind the counter on a wall were rows of wooden boxes marked with numbers. Jake DeBragga was postmaster, but when he went out to fish, his wife took charge, while their daughter ran the store. Jake's wife was round, pink-cheeked, and, most days, smiled and talked at length, to everyone. Some summer people joked about her, saying she was a chronic gossip, but they liked her anyway.

Today, when she saw Anne, she looked away and shuffled papers on the desk. When at last she did turn back, she frowned and said, "How are you, Anne?"

Anne tried to think what might have happened yesterday. Had she hurt her feelings somehow? Surely not. As she looked across the counter at their box, she saw a light blue envelope. "Another letter from my dad."

Jake's wife picked up her pen and drew a circle on a

pad. "It seems to be from someone else." She glanced at Anne. "Where's your mother?"

"On the hill. Here, I'll take it up to her."

As Jake's wife handed her the letter, she said softly, "Looks important. Here, you'll have to sign for it." She handed Anne a slip of paper and her pen. "Sign right here." When Anne had signed, Jake's wife said, "Give it to her right away."

Anne turned away and, as she did so, looked down at the envelope. The address was badly typed. She turned it over. On the back, she saw a printed name and, underneath it, an address.

Lieut. Cmdr. James J. Cooke, Chaplain, U.S.N.
Box 1112
Brooklyn Navy Yard
Brooklyn, N.Y.

Anne's heart began to pound. Once, she had heard her mother say, "I hope a chaplain never comes to call on us." She knew that chaplains brought bad news.

As she walked across the room, Anne's fingers tightened on the letter. In the sun-baked parking lot, she stood alone, staring at a lobsterman aboard his boat, rocking on a gentle surge. Jake's pier was just around the corner of the building. Maybe Jake would be there now. Jake could tell her what to do.

Jake's boat was gone. Anne sat on a shelving rock that overlooked a little pool, thinking of her mother, on the hill alone, waiting for her Uncle Ted. Anne shut her eyes. Sunlight filtered through her eyelids, making patterns in her brain.

Opening her eyes again, she saw the letter in her hand. The thing to do was tear it into strips and— Better still, why not burn it? If she burned it, she could make it disappear. As she stood up, she saw Jake's boat coming toward her, but instead of waiting for him, she retreated to the parking lot. Her knees were weak, but she drifted toward the store and pulled the screen door open wide enough so she could step inside. Jake's wife was out of sight behind the counter. Anne stood beside a glass display case while Jake's daughter, dark and stocky, finished waiting on a skinny, gray-haired woman. As if surprised to see her back, Jake's daughter said, "Hi. What can I do for you?"

Anne studied the case. Camels, Lucky Strikes, and Chesterfields. *Chesterfields.* Those were what Anne's father smoked.

"We can't sell you cigarettes."

Anne shook her head. She said, "No." She almost smiled. "I'd like some matches, please. My dad—I mean, my mother uses them to light our stove."

"Then you'll want the wooden ones."

"No. I'd like a folder, please."

Jake's daughter reached into a wicker basket. "These are free."

Anne nodded absently. "Thanks," she said. She turned around and went back out, started walking toward the narrow path that led to where her mother was. She stopped and stared ahead of her, turned aside, and waded through a stand of grass. She knelt down on a little beach and put the letter on the sand. A gust of wind turned it over, picked it up, and blew it toward a scattering of broken shells. Anne retrieved it, dug a hole, and dropped

63

the letter into it. She flipped the cover of the folder back, bent a match and tore it off. She struck the match. The flame flared, settled down and burned. Anne shielded it and watched it as it traveled toward her fingers, followed closely by an ember. She made no move to burn the letter. She stared at it until the flame began to singe her fingers, then let go and watched the match fall on the sand, curling, twisting. As it died, a puff of smoke rose up from it, became a plume, and disappeared.

She swallowed hard and moved back through the grass with the letter in her hand. She started up the hill again. Her mother's back was turned and she was waving joyfully, pointing to an empty dock. Anne, suddenly aware that if her mother turned she'd see the letter, folded it and stuffed it into her hip pocket.

5

Anne watched her mother moving toward a zigzag path that led down to the waterfront. As she went, she caught a glimpse of Anne. She called to her to come along.

Instead of following her mother, Anne stood still and watched the boat sail into port. Aunt Adelaide stood by the mast, while Uncle Ted, relaxed but concentrating on his sailing, rounded up and headed for the empty dock, where Anne's mother stood and waited. Aunt Adelaide pulled down the jib and took a docking line in hand. Anne heard her call, "Alice, you look wonderful!"

Anne felt a tightness in her chest. The sun, reflecting

in the waters of the harbor, hurt her eyes. She felt like running down the hill and screaming, telling them that nothing mattered anymore. She clenched her fists and watched as Uncle Ted reached up and pulled the mainsail down, furled it loosely, tied a stop around it, and began to help Aunt Adelaide fend off and dock the boat.

Anne saw her mother step aboard the boat, kiss Aunt Adelaide, and give her Uncle Ted a hug. When she turned to look at Anne, her mother stared, then stepped ashore. She started walking up the path, and when she was close enough to see her daughter's face, she gave a cry, "Anne! What is it?"

Anne stood straight. Defiantly she looked into her mother's eyes. As her mother's face grew stern, Anne turned and ran away, moving up the hill. Her mother scrambled after her. Her voice was shrill. "Come back. You must!"

Anne was nimble, but her mother was determined to catch up, and on the bluff, she caught her wrist and pulled her back. Then, all at once, she gave her such a violent shove that Anne fell down. "Anne!" she shouted. "Please don't torture me like this!"

Frightened, trembling, Anne reached up, took her mother's hand, and, in a thin voice, said, "I didn't mean to torture you."

Her mother, stricken, knelt and took her in her arms. "You can't keep it to yourself. Now tell me what's the matter."

Anne reached around and, as she felt the letter in her pocket, whispered, "Mom. It's—"

"Yes, I know. It's serious." Again her mother lost control. "Give it to me now," she screamed.

SEA CHANGE

Aunt Adelaide appeared and, looking anxious, said, "I'm glad to see you, Anne."

Anne's voice was flat and barely audible. "Hello," she said.

"Goodness, it can't be as bad as that. If you quarreled, you can—"

Anne pulled the letter out. Her mother stared at it. As she took the envelope, she trembled, visibly. She read the name and address on the back, took a deep breath, closed her eyes, and, frowning, tore off a corner of the envelope. With an angry stab, she slit it end to end, and pulled the letter out. As she read, her expression underwent an awful change. Her mouth twitched, once. She let go of the envelope, which fluttered, brushed against a clump of grass, and blew away.

Aunt Adelaide went after it, picked it up, and glanced at it. Her lips grew white. Anne's mother pushed the letter toward Aunt Adelaide, who took it from her, held it with the envelope, and fumbled in a canvas bag she carried on a string around her waist. She pulled out a pair of horn-rimmed glasses and, with deft, deliberate motions, put them on. As Aunt Adelaide began to read, Anne's mother turned her back to them. Then she bowed her head and wept.

Anne wished that she could put her arms around her mother but she knew she couldn't move. She felt exactly as she had when she had had her tonsils out, as she had looked into the face of the anesthetist and seen her smiling down at her. The deep blue sky and sunlit grass seemed to swim and swirl around her, and the thought of standing up made her choke and gasp for breath.

In a ghostly, pleading voice, Anne's mother said, "Adelaide, don't go away."

"I'm not going anywhere." She slipped the letter and its envelope into her bag. Just then, Uncle Ted's voice came from somewhere on the path. "Hello up there. Where are you all?" He approached them carelessly, walking like somebody half his age. "You're beautiful, the three of you. I'm lucky to—"

Aunt Adelaide turned and faced him. "Ted," she said. "We have some news." She touched his arm. He stood absolutely still, studying Anne's mother's tear-streaked face, before he stepped across the grass and stood beside her. In a deep and quiet voice, he said, to no one in particular, "I think I've guessed. I hope I'm wrong."

Adelaide turned to Anne. "Was it you who fetched the mail?"

"Yes. It was."

Aunt Adelaide said, "Someone ought to tell you straight. Your father died three weeks ago. The chaplain went to your apartment in New York, two times, then found out where your mother was."

Softly, Uncle Ted asked, "Is there any doubt at all?"

"No, Ted."

Uncle Ted sat on the grass. Turning to Anne's mother, he said gently, "We'll stay here a week or so. We'll do some sailing, if you like."

Anne's mother nodded. "Maybe. Yes." The sun was high, and as she looked at him, she squinted, almost smiled. "I'm glad you're here."

"So am I."

"Please talk to me. It doesn't matter what you say."

67

Uncle Ted looked at the ground, reached up, and pulled the collar of his shirt. He drew a deep breath. Adelaide sat down near Anne, touched her shoulder, took her hand. Anne blurted, "Tell me what it means."

Aunt Adelaide spoke very softly. "What does what mean?"

Forming words one at a time, Anne asked, "What does it mean that I can't cry?"

Aunt Adelaide hesitated. "I'm not sure. Would you like to take a walk?"

Anne nodded. "Yes."

Uncle Ted said, "Come back soon."

They got up, walked together through an empty field, and approached a second hill that overlooked a little beach, washed by small waves. Anne sat down. "I didn't really want to walk."

"Nor did I, but we had to leave them to themselves. They go back as far as people can go back."

Below them, on the little beach, three mothers and their children sat together on a blanket on the sand. One was a kind of commissar, talking loudly, handing out the food and drinks. The children, like a flight of buntings come to rest, pecking, pulling, giving voice to hunger and frustration, finally settled down to eat. Anne heard the engine of a fishing boat rapping out a steady beat, its echoes rising from the waters of the harbor, coughing, dying, leaving an unwelcome silence. The branches of a nearby tree moved almost imperceptibly and a vagrant puff of wind streaked the waters of the sound. Anne was sure that if she went down to the beach and walked past where the people sat, she would be invisible, and if she spoke, they wouldn't hear. She was suddenly afraid. Timidly she stretched her hand out to Aunt Adelaide. In a broken voice, she asked, "Why don't you speak?"

Aunt Adelaide touched her hand. "You were a thousand miles away. I didn't want to interrupt—"

"I wasn't really far away. It's just—I feel cut off from everything."

"From me?"

"A little. I don't know. I'd hate it if you went away."

"I won't."

"Good. That's good."

Aunt Adelaide picked up a stick and, with it, drew a line across a sandy patch of soil. "We don't really need to talk."

"At least, I'd like to hear you talk." She paused. "Do you love Mom?"

"I love your mother very much. I love you both."

"I *wanted* to leave Mom just now. I wish I hadn't wanted to."

"It's just as well. What could the four of us have talked about?"

Anne clenched her fists. "I hate my mother now."

Aunt Adelaide gave a glimmer of a frown. Then she smiled and, in a reassuring way, pressed Anne's hand. "She'll soon be strong enough to try to understand your feelings. Now she has to try to understand her own. It must be the same for you. In time, you'll start to share your pain."

Down on the beach, two boys appeared and tossed a football to each other. One hunched over, running, dodging, then straightened up, and threw a pass. The other reached up, missed, and sprawled. His laughter, racketing above the beach, made Anne angry. How could anybody laugh?

Aunt Adelaide's voice came as if from far away. Softly she repeated something she had said before: "Your mother and your Uncle Ted go back as far as people can go back." Anne glanced at her and Aunt Adelaide went on. "Uncle Ted goes to church and sometimes I go with him but I've never had a faith. I suppose I may be sorry, someday. Anyway, I shock him when I say I half believe in something Hindus think is so. It seems to me no accident that people like your mother and your Uncle Ted are especially close to each other. Someone who believes that souls live into eternity, in different bodies, might say that they were old souls, that they might have loved each other in another time and place."

"Am I an old soul, do you think?"

"Maybe. Yes, I think you are."

"If I am, then you are, too."

Aunt Adelaide gave Anne a long and loving look. "Did your mother ever tell you how she hated me when we first met?"

"I don't know. I think she did."

"It wasn't long before we saw that we weren't enemies at all. I remember, at the end of that first day, after we had made a truce and seen that we would soon be friends, your mother said that she and I were troublemakers."

"Were you really troublemakers?"

"I think we were. That day we were. When I married Uncle Ted, I settled down. I'm different now."

Smiling faintly, looking arch, Anne said, "Are you?"

Aunt Adelaide laughed. "Right you are. I haven't really changed at all. I'm much the same."

Anne gave a gasping sob and Aunt Adelaide embraced her. Anne, trembling, pressed her face against Aunt Adelaide's shirt front. Her tears welled up and overflowed.

6

When they went home, Anne stayed outdoors. At first she sat down on the pier. Then she wandered in the dunes, sometimes glancing toward the house. Her mother lay on a deck chair, staring out at the horizon. Sometimes Uncle Ted came out, for several minutes at a time. Anne watched her mother, but she knew she didn't want to talk to her, at least not yet. In the car, coming back from Menemsha, her mother had looked straight at her and Anne had had to turn away.

Later, Anne approached the porch and, seeing her mother, said, "Hello, Mom."

"Come sit with me."

Anne went over, climbed the steps, and sat down in a wicker chair. "How are you, Mom?"

Her mother shrugged. "At the moment, feeling sick. I'm restless, but when I begin to get up, I feel dizzy. I can't bring myself to care about the things I cared about. I'm not sure I want to care."

"That's how I feel." Parroting Aunt Adelaide, Anne said, "We'll soon begin to share our pain."

"I hope so, Anne."

71

Anne knew she couldn't tell her mother that she felt light-years away from her and that she couldn't think about the reasons why.

The screen door creaked and Uncle Ted looked down on them. "I'm going shopping. Adelaide will stay with you."

Anne's mother said, "That's fine, Ted. Drive carefully."

He glanced at Anne. "I wonder if you'd like to come."

Anne brightened. "Yes. I can help you carry things."

They walked together to the car. Uncle Ted ducked down and slid into the driver's seat. He waved Anne in. At first, Anne felt a mild resentment that he acted not as if someone had died but as if she'd stubbed her toe or caught a cold. He asked, "Is that man Jake reliable?"

"Of course he is."

Earlier that afternoon, when they had come down from the hill above Menemsha and had walked across the parking lot, Jake must have seen them from the store. He had known about the letter. He'd come out and told Anne's mother he was sorry. It had been an awkward moment for them all. After that, Uncle Ted had taken Jake aside and talked to him about his boat, about the tides and how the lines should be adjusted. Jake had said he'd mind the boat. Now Anne said, "Jake's a good man. He's a friend."

"Good. I won't fret about the boat." Uncle Ted drove with something close to recklessness. On the road above the bluffs, he headed east. In Edgartown, they moved down the long main street, toward the yacht club and the harbor. All at once, Uncle Ted, kind and handsome as he was, seemed an arrogant impostor. Anne's father should be sitting in the driver's seat. The thought made tears well up again. They streaked her cheeks and wet her shirt. One escaped and settled on her collarbone. It tickled and she reached up and blotted it.

Uncle Ted parked the car. He set the brake, glanced at Anne, and, with a linen handkerchief, dried her tears.

Summer people moved along the sidewalk, tan and smiling, wearing shorts and tennis shirts. Three of Anne's schoolmates from New York City lived here summers with their parents. One of them, Heather Brown, had spent a day with Anne last week. Anne knew that, if she saw a friend, she'd want to run away, because she couldn't talk about her father and she couldn't act as if this day was just like any other day. Uncle Ted asked, "Can I help?"

"I don't think so."

"You can stay here if you like."

"I want to help you carry things."

He smiled. "I'll make two trips." He took out his shopping list. "We need oranges and eggs and cereal. I want bacon. We need things that go with lobsters. Adelaide said baked potatoes might be nice. Do you like peas?"

"I like *canned* peas."

"Adelaide would guillotine me if I brought back something canned. She likes fresh things. Do you like beans?"

"Lima beans?"

"I was thinking of string beans."

"You mean you don't like lima beans?"

"I think I like string beans better."

"Lima beans are tastier."

Uncle Ted began to laugh. "This is ridiculous," he said. He gave her a sidelong glance. "I'll be right back."

"I'll go with you. I hate sitting in the car."

Uncle Ted was not a shopper. For him, the A&P was a maze lined with banks of cans and bottles, cuts of meat in slanting cases, paper goods, bins of fruits and vegetables. Anne helped him shop. He apologized for buying so much. "We'll need supplies to put aboard the boat," he said.

Anne felt a sudden rush of fear. "I thought you said you'd stay a week."

"We will, at least a week. It's just that we'll be going sailing now and then."

"Is there an ice chest on your boat?"

"Indeed there is."

"Good. Jake sells ice."

"Fine. Let's get going." They had five bags of groceries. Anne carried two and Uncle Ted, with the help of a boy who cleaned the bins and swept the floors, took the rest. In the car, Uncle Ted said, "Show me to the lobster pound."

On the way back to the house, they passed a meadow where a herd of sheep was grazing. "Uncle Ted?"

"What is it, Anne?"

"I'd like to stop around this curve. There's a place beside a gate where you can park."

Uncle Ted pulled off the road. The crow's feet at the corners of his eyes crinkled as he said, "Now what?"

"I know this will make me sad but I want to do it anyway." She pulled the handle, pushed the door, and

74

stepped into a patch of grass. "You come, too." Not looking back to see if he was following, Anne walked toward
a little pond. She had come here several times with her
father, to admire a pair of orange-billed white swans
which spent their summers paddling on the quiet waters.
They were still here, near a stand of tall marsh grass.
Anne saw that something had been added. A cygnet,
brown and fluffy, floated near the larger birds. Anne sat
down. Uncle Ted came along and stood beside her. He
sat down, putting his arm around her shoulders in a
gentle, natural way, and hugged her. The largest swan
led his mate in their direction and the cygnet followed,
beady-eyed. The necks of the two adult birds moved in
graceful, undulating curves. As he approached his visitors,
the leader chose to arch his neck and raise his bill. Anne
said, "He's like a strong and noble gladiator." Uncle Ted
gave her another hug, and because he didn't speak, she
said. "How come you understand so well?"

"I lost someone long ago. I remember how it felt. I
feel it still."

"I'm afraid I won't remember."

"You will, Anne."

"Who did you lose, Uncle Ted?"

"A young woman, someone I loved very much."

"I think I remember now. The locket you gave Mom
when she was young belonged to her."

"That's right. It did."

The adult swans grew tired of looking at them, turned
around, and paddled off. The cygnet followed, giving
Anne a backward glance. Idly, Anne picked up a pebble
and tossed it into the shallow water near her feet. She

watched the concentric circles grow until, at last, they disappeared. "Aunt Adelaide said there wasn't any doubt. Still, there might be some mistake."

"About your father's death you mean?"

"Yes. I've heard of things like that."

"So have I. But there appears to be no doubt."

"How did he die?"

"Are you sure you want to know?"

Anne pressed her lips together, hard. "Yes. I'm sure."

"It was in the North Sea someplace. His destroyer escort was attacked by fighter planes. He and the second mate were shot. Your father died."

"What— What did the captain do with him?"

"What your father would have wanted."

"I know. He had a hero's burial, at sea. I like to think that all the seas belong to him." When Anne turned to Uncle Ted, she saw tears streaming down his cheeks. She said, "Men aren't supposed to cry. I'm glad you're crying, Uncle Ted."

7

They sat around the kitchen table, faces in the candle-light. Anne had thought that supper would be almost more than she could bear, but so far she hadn't cried. Before they had begun to eat, Uncle Ted had bowed his head. He'd kept the blessing very short. "Please, God, bless and keep us all."

After they finished, while Uncle Ted cleared away the lobster shells, Anne's mother spoke. "Thank you for the dinner, Ted. Sorry I just ate one claw."

"We'll keep the rest. You can have it cold tomorrow."

As Anne took off the dinner plates, Aunt Adelaide said, "Now dessert. We have ice cream."

Even in the soft, warm light, Anne's mother's face was empty, drawn. Underneath her red-rimmed eyes were bluish pouches. As if listening to sounds nobody else could hear, she cocked her head. At last she said, "Anne and I—I think it was yesterday. Could it have been? We picked a lot of blueberries. We had— I don't think I want ice cream. I want blueberries instead." She nodded. "Yes. With milk."

Anne heard what sounded like the hinges of the screen door creaking. No, how could they be? She hadn't heard a car come in, and anyway, who would come to see them now? She tried to speak but made no sound. Someone knocked. Uncle Ted moved toward the door. He touched the knob and asked, "Who's there?"

They heard a voice. Uncle Ted turned the knob, and as he pulled the door back, Anne saw Gary standing there. She could see that he was frightened. She said, "Gary?"

"Yes," he whispered.

"Come on in."

He stepped inside. He fidgeted. Anne repeated, "Come on in." Then she said, "We have blueberries and ice cream."

He pressed his hand against his crew-necked Shetland sweater, closed his eyes, and said explosively, "I heard

77

about—" His eyelids flickered and he stared. "I came because I thought you'd like to take a walk. I mean, with someone your own age. If you wouldn't—"

"Yes, I would."

Uncle Ted sat down again. He frowned at Gary, but Anne's mother smiled and said, "Be careful when you cross the pond." Then her expression changed. She gave Anne a frightened glance. "Please don't swim."

"I won't. Don't worry, Mom."

Gary's voice cracked. "I thought Anne might want to talk. I mean, of course we won't go swimming."

"Does your mother know you're here?"

"No," Gary said. "I told her I was going walking. I don't think—" He reddened. "I don't think she worries much."

Adelaide said, "Have dessert when you come back."

Gary backed up, and together they went out. Anne led the way around the house and down the path. Gary didn't say a word. On the pier, Anne asked him, "Do you want to row?"

"Sure. I'll row."

With her foot, Anne reached out and pulled the skiff in, stepped aboard the little boat, and, working hard to keep her balance, climbed across a thwart. She sat down and, leaning forward, put her elbows on her knees.

The waters of the pond were black. The oars made little tails of white, and once, Anne saw a bright, fluorescent flash. Overhead, the sky was clear and deep blue now. They beached the boat and walked across the nearest dune. Anne pointed toward the cliff. "Let's go that way, okay?"

"Sure."

They walked several feet apart, at first not saying anything. When Anne spoke again, she said, "Last night seems days and weeks away."

"I know."

"How could you know?"

"I remember."

Anne stopped walking. "What do you remember, Gary?"

"Let's not talk about it yet."

"Okay." She moved along. She raised her chin, as if responding to a challenge, and looked beyond the cresting waves. Her voice rose just above the lamentations of the sand. "I love the sea."

She saw him grinning. "So do I."

As they approached the cliff, she gestured. "Let's climb up it."

They moved toward an overhang and found a little notch where they could scramble to the top. Below them, waves attacked the rocks, shattered, sent up plumes of white. Staring at a dark and isolated pool, Anne shuddered slightly. Gary, head bowed, stood as if he might be marshaling his courage. Anne sat down. As Gary settled down beside her, Anne said awkwardly, "I guess—I mean, thanks for coming over."

Gary laughed. "I was frightened half to death."

"Of me?"

"No, of your mother and the others." Then, as if afraid he might delay, he spoke. "I can tell you now," he said. "My brother died three months ago. He was killed in the Pacific, in the battle of Midway."

"Gary. No."

"He was in the navy, too."

"How come you never mentioned it?"

"Until today, we'd never talked. I'd never really had a chance."

"You were brave to come tonight. I bet you'd never have come if your brother—I mean, I guess that's why you came."

"Maybe so."

The stars were bright, seemed almost close enough to touch. The Milky Way cut its swath across their shoulders, disappearing in the south. Pointing, Anne said, "Look at that star. It's the brightest of them all."

"That's Altair. My brother taught me all about the stars. He was handy with a sextant. He taught me how to shoot the sun. That's not hard. He could take a star sight, too."

"Did you love him very much?"

"Yes." Gazing upward at the sky, Gary said, "It's hard to believe that he is gone. It hurts to think that I could search the milky way and voyage to the farthest star and never find him anywhere."

"My father isn't *gone*. I don't believe that." Anne was silent for a moment, and then she spoke again. "This afternoon, Aunt Adelaide told me that Hindus believe that souls keep living."

"Most people believe that souls live on. I guess I loved my brother's soul, but I *know* I loved his face and I liked to watch his hands when he used tools and instruments. I wish you could have watched him work."

Anne had to wait to speak. She whispered, "Yes, I loved my father's face."

"It's funny. Sometimes I look at photographs, but I've

found that they can get in the way. Remembering is best. Memories come all by themselves."

Anne nodded solemnly. "It's nice to have a friend like you."

8

Gary left her at the back door. "Tell your mom I've had dessert."

"Good night, Gary."

"See you, Anne."

Inside, Anne found her mother sitting in a wicker chair, feet up on another chair, staring at an open book. Anne said, "Hi, Mom."

"Hello, Anne." She pointed to a crack of light underneath Ted and Adelaide's bedroom door. "They must be reading."

Anne sat down. "May I stay up a little while?"

"Of course you can." She shut her book. "I haven't read a single word. No, that's not true. I read one line a dozen times."

"I haven't even tried to read."

Anne's mother took her glasses off, folded them, and put them on a nearby table, lenses up. "This afternoon is all a blur, an awful, nightmare memory, but I know that I was cruel."

"Cruel to me?"

"Yes, cruel to you."

"It's okay. Really, Mom. I should have given you the letter right away. It was just—"

"Let's forgive each other, Anne."

"Sure, Mom." Remembering her talk with Uncle Ted this afternoon, Anne said, "I never really understood your love for Uncle Ted until today. I mean, I've always loved him, too, but now I see what you see, what you saw when you were young."

Anne's mother gave her first real smile since she'd read the chaplain's letter. "Good. I'm glad." She seemed about to speak again but looked away.

"What is it, Mom?"

"I'm not sure. I'm very tired. Thoughts fly by and disappear. I think they're lost, but they come back."

Anne nodded. "Uncle Ted told me everything he knew. I mean, he told me how Dad died. It helped a lot."

"I almost wish I'd *lived* his death."

"You mean you wish you'd been there with him?"

"Yes, I do. If he could take it, so could I."

"You really mean it, don't you, Mom?"

"Of course I do."

"Dad died a hero's death."

Her mother stared down at the cover of her book. At last, she said, "Yes, I guess so."

"Aren't you sure?"

As if talking to herself, Anne's mother said, "I don't know what a hero is. He went to war to fight against what seems to all of us an evil force. He was brave, but at the end, if he had any time at all to contemplate his death, he was probably afraid." Her face was suddenly contorted. "God forgive me. I should be protecting you.

82

Instead, I'm thinking of myself. You see, I need to face it all and stare it down."

"I'm old enough to hear the truth."

"I admire you very much."

"Me, Mom?"

"Yes, you. You're just like him."

"No, I'm not. Anyway, I don't want to be admired. Mom?"

"Yes."

"Let's have a service in New York. Was Dad religious?"

"You know as well as I do, Anne. No, not in any formal sense. He believed in God."

"I'd like a military service, wouldn't you? I know his captain had a service on the ship, but even so, when we have ours, I'd like to have his shipmates there."

"Yes. Let's do that, even if we have to wait. He was fond of Captain Tripp. He often talked about the men."

"I want someone to play taps."

"We'd better find a good musician. Every note must be—" Tears filled her eyes.

Anne got up and knelt beside her mother's chair. Her mother sat up straight and hugged her. "I love you, not because you're just like him." She laughed. "In many ways, you're more like me." She kissed Anne's cheek, leaned back, and said, "It's strange. I'm happy, almost happy, at the end of this sad day."

"So am I. Daddy's close to us tonight."

The Bridge

I

Lisa ran along the cracked and slanting concrete side-walk of a narrow Brooklyn street, jumped across a pile of litter, dodged a jogger, and kept going. High above her rose a tower of the bridge, its Gothic arches touched by warm October light. Moving down a short, dark slope, she mounted several sets of steps to gain the concrete ramp leading to the wooden walkway.

Her mother's fear was like an octopean arm, reaching from the house on West Tenth Street, across the roof-tops of New York, across Soho and Chinatown, to prod and tease the panic rising in Lisa's breast. I'm late, she thought. I'm very late.

Most times, the bridge was hers, an arching pathway to serene and happy hours. The benches on its walkway were retreats where, on good days, she and Aaron sat and talked. This afternoon, she'd gone with him to Brooklyn Heights, where he lived. They'd walked along the promenade that overlooked a set of piers where freighters docked. Not until she'd started back had she thought about what time it was.

Now, on the bridge, she wished that she could clear the span in half a dozen giant steps. As she ran, dark hair streaming, she could hear the steady whine of cars below her, see a stroboscopic flash as a taxicab went by, as if in angry flight, above the waters of the river. A tugboat, with barge in tow, moved downstream, to intersect the wakes of ferryboats converging on the Battery.

Stopping, drawing breath, then moving toward the middle of the bridge, Lisa turned to catch a fleeting glimpse of New York's Upper Bay, a plateau under dappled cloud, marked with intermittent bands of gray and streaks of light like scatterings of freshly pulverized green glass. The glare was bright enough to make her shift her gaze to a cluster of surviving buildings, relics of a bygone time. Lisa paused to catch her breath. It must be 6:15, at least. Her mother would be wild by now and Lisa might not make it to Tenth Street for half an hour, maybe more. She broke into a run again.

The sun appeared below a cloud, telling her that daylight wouldn't fade quite yet. Lisa, breathless, chanted softly to herself, "Gotta move. Move it girl." Running past a loving couple and a man with a flattened nose and eyes that gleamed in narrow slits, she covered a deserted stretch and approached a boy eighteen or so, who stared at her as if to draw her into his dark fantasies. Looking older than her years, she was used to things like that, but since the two of them were separated from the others on the bridge by at least a hundred yards, her stomach did a little flip. She raised her chin and gave the boy a chilly look.

88

On the Manhattan side, the concrete ramp ended in an entrance to a subway station which consisted of a filthy wonderland of corridors and turnstiles, platforms, tracks. Lisa, supple, moving like a ballet dancer through the crowds, remembered that she'd left her student pass at school. She dug into a pocket of her jeans, hoping she would find a subway token among her coins. Feeling what she thought was one, she pulled it out. No. A quarter. Fish again. She found a token, chose a turnstile, waited while a woman with an elephantine rear squeezed past its prongs. On the platform, Lisa fidgeted and paced, watching for a train's headlights. When they came, they trembled, moving bug-eyed toward the platform. Lisa stepped back, thinking of a recent headline, WOMAN KILLED BY SUBWAY TRAIN, WAS PUSHED OR FELL.

At Fourteenth Street, the platforms and the stairways were alive with people pushing, running. Passing tanks of colored drinks and a garish pretzel stand, Lisa surfaced. Looking west, she saw a violet afterglow, a traffic light, red at first, then green above a hooded rectangle which sheltered the command to WALK.

On Thirteenth Street, Lisa passed a little shop whose name she liked, Les Trois Petits Cochons, crossed the street, and, running down Fifth Avenue, stopped at Tenth Street, waiting for the light to change.

2

The façade of Lisa's house, red brick, white trim, its lower windows tall behind its flower boxes, loomed above her. Slowing down, she climbed the steps, pulled out her keys, slid one into the top lock, and, as she turned it, heard someone inside the house release the lower lock. Lisa pocketed her keys. The door swung open. Her mother's face was pale. "Come in," she said.

"I'm coming in."

"Where have you been?"

"I'm sorry, Mom. I should have called."

"Yes, you should have. I've talked to several of your friends."

Annoyed that her mother had called her friends, Lisa said, "I'm glad you didn't call the police."

"Don't joke about it. As it is—"

"As it is, you're angry at me."

"Frightened, angry, what's the difference? I came home from work at one. Most days, you come home at three. At four, I started—"

"Stop it, Mom. I've heard it all a thousand times." Lisa hung her jacket up in the hall closet, moved as if to climb the stairs. "Let me go up and take a shower."

Her mother frowned. "All right. Just tell me where you've been."

Lisa stopped. She glared and shouted, "I've been walking."

Lisa's mother, shaken, said, "Don't scream at me."

Lisa sat down on the stairs. "I'm sorry, Mom. Look, I'm fine. I mean, I haven't been in danger."

"There's always danger in New York. I don't have to tell you that."

"No, you don't." She stared down at her running shoes. Their toes were black. Insistently she told her mother, "If the city frightens you, we'd better move to a suburban paradise, where everything is neat and clean and everyone is bored to death."

"Nonsense, Lisa. We *belong* in New York City. All I ask is, when you know you're coming home as late as this, give me a call."

Lisa stood up. "If I'd called you, right away I'd have had to tell you where I was and then—" She sighed. "You ask a lot of questions, Mom."

"All you have to do is answer."

Lisa, irritated still, said, "No. That's not all I have to do. It doesn't matter what I say. You keep pressing me for more. It's—"

Suddenly her mother asked, "What happened to your backpack, Lisa?"

"It's at school. Mom, try to understand. I'm so innocent it *hurts*."

"That's exactly why I worry."

Lisa glared. "I can change things in a hurry if you really want me to." She turned and pounded up the stairs. On the second floor she listened, thinking she would hear her mother call to her. When she didn't, Lisa wheeled and, passing what they called the TV room, climbed a second set of stairs, went to her room, flicked the light switch, slammed the door, and lay down on her bed.

Her walls were lined with abstract paintings she had done, some suggesting sunlit seascapes, others somber, almost spectral. In a dark corner was a photograph of victims of the Hiroshima bombing. When she'd hung the photograph, she'd made her mother think that there was something *wrong* with her. She wished her mother wouldn't brood. Staring upward at the ceiling, which was cracked and had been patched, she whispered, "The injustice of it all. Look at Julie Middleton." At fourteen, Julie acted like a fool. She flirted, teased, and tortured boys. She smoked pot. At home and on the street, she swore. Her mother didn't care what Julie did. Lisa didn't want to *be* like Julie Middleton, but she wished she had the kind of freedom Julie had.

Lisa got up and stood at one of her two windows, looking down. Their garden was a battleground for cats. Pigeons roosted on the fences. She pulled down one shade, then the other. She took off her running shoes, tossed her jeans across her bed, put on her robe, and left the room. In the hall, she looked down the narrow slot between the banisters. All she heard were clicking sounds, as her mother set the table. The door to Ted's room stood wide open. Her brother, Ted, a senior at Columbia, came home sometimes, but mostly he lived with his girl, who had a place on Broadway near 100th Street, above a Szechwan restaurant. At home, he had the front bedroom, which was almost twice the size of Lisa's room and, on good days, was light and sunny.

In the shower, Lisa brooded. She knew what her mother had been trying to say downstairs, about the reason why she worried. Mom knew she was *innocent*, which somehow made her prey to all the evils of New York. But Lisa wasn't often careless. She figured in a pinch she'd know what to do. As she washed, she frowned. She'd never kept important secrets, not until that day last spring when Aaron had sat down beside her in a subway car and started talking. Right away, she'd seen that he was different from the other boys. He was smarter, more mature. At school, she'd scarcely noticed him. Tall and skinny, with curly hair and wearing circular, metal-rimmed glasses, he'd seemed a shy, retiring *brain*.

Lisa left the shower stall and dried herself. She said aloud, "Aaron's great. He's a friend."

Back in her room, she dressed again. Putting on her running shoes, she sat down in a little chair. When she stood up, she found that she was facing Bear, who, looking like a Muslim potentate, was flanked by dolls of many nations given Lisa by Aunt Adelaide, who was ninety-six last month. Bear had belonged to Lisa's grandmother. Feeling like a child again, she spoke to him. "*You* understand. It's just that I don't want them all to know how I spend every minute of my time. I mean, I'm entitled to at least *one* secret, don't you think?"

Bear's eyes gleamed. A fold of worn, still faintly furry cloth hung loose above his left eye, making him look very wise.

In the kitchen, Lisa said to her mother, "I'm sorry I blew up at you. You just have to trust me, Mom."

Her mother shook her head and said, "You've always been so absolutely forthright, Lisa. I don't see—" Hearing someone at the door, she went out to the hall and waited. "Hello, Gary."

Lisa, hanging back, watched them hugging. "Hello, Dad."

Lisa's father was a little overweight. He beamed at her, took off his hat, and dropped it on a chair. "I'll go wash up. I don't want another drink. I had two with Charlie Bissell."

Her mother said, "Okay, we'll put dinner on."

"Is Ted coming home tomorrow?"

"Yes. With Gina. After supper, Gina's leaving, going to Connecticut."

Lisa's father hugged her tight. In order to disarm them both, Lisa almost told her father that she'd been a wicked child, had failed to call when she knew she'd be home late. Instead, she said, "I hope you walked around at noon. You know, on the Battery. It was beautiful today."

When her father went upstairs and they could hear the water running, Lisa's mother asked her, "Were you on the Battery?"

Lisa had an urge to tease her mother, tell her she'd been to the South Bronx, to look at some of the deserted tenements but she said, "No. Not today."

3

After she had done her homework, Lisa went to bed. She read awhile before she heard her father coming up. She gave her hair a little pat and sat against her pillows, with her sheet and her electric blanket pulled up to her waist. Her father's voice came from the hall. "May I come in?"

"Sure. I'm in bed."

He'd taken off his dark gray suit and put on a pair of khakis, worn Top-Siders and a crew-necked Shetland sweater. He sat against her brass footboard. Lisa said, "I have three pillows. Here. Take one."

"Thanks. That's better."

"How's Wall Street?"

"Sly old thing. You've never asked me that before." Winking, he said, "Wall Street's fine. I work mornings and I spend my afternoons with business friends in restaurants whose walls are paneled in dark wood, where the tablecloths are white and drinks are served on silver trays."

Lisa smiled. "Of all your business friends, which one do you like most, Dad?"

"Charlie Bissell."

"How come, Dad?"

"Most of them begin with pleasantries, sneak up on business, and, once started, talk of nothing else. Charlie gets right down to brass tacks, finishes in nothing flat, and after that, we talk about what matters—books, art, music, things like that."

"Do you look forward to your lunches and your drinks with Mr. Bissell?"

"Yes, I do. What makes you ask?"

"It's just that I think friendships like that, good ones, are important. Don't you, Dad?"

"Lisa?"

"Yes, Dad."

When he smiled, she thought that he must be the kindest man who ever lived. "It seems you have a secret life."

Glancing at him, Lisa said, "Yes, Papa, I've become the mistress of a dark Italian count. I know he's absolutely worthless, but I love him desperately. He's so— how to put it? He's a devastating man, handsome, charming—"

"Is the man a citizen?"

"A citizen? You mean a *U.S.* citizen? I've never asked. Must you be provincial, Papa?"

"Your move, Lisa."

"Okay, Dad. Last June, I met a boy named Aaron Newman. He's a class ahead of me. I'd seen him lots of times before but hadn't really talked to him. He's a little goofy-looking."

"Sounds like me."

"In some ways. Yes."

"Do you love him?"

"*Love* him? Are you crazy, Dad?"

"Okay. Sorry. You spent the afternoon with him and came home late."

"I've spent at least two afternoons a week with him since I went back to school last month. We don't meet on rainy days."

"You mean, if it starts to rain, you call your date off. Really, that's ridiculous."

Lisa laughed. "No, Dad. We don't make *dates*. Aaron kind of watches for me, en route to the subway station."

"I don't suppose you watch for him."

Lisa smiled. "Sometimes I do. Most of my friends walk

to school. You know. They're Upper East Side kids. We both take the IRT."

"Where does your friend Aaron live?"

"In Brooklyn Heights."

"Do you and he hang around with other kids?"

"No. It's been a secret friendship."

"Why?"

"Really, Dad. You're so naïve. It's boring being with tons of kids, and parents always mess things up. Parents try to *structure* things."

He said sadly, "So they do."

"Dad, I love you very much." Lisa sat up very straight. "Is Mom happy, do you think?"

"Mostly. Yes. Working with autistic kids, even part-time, can be tiring and discouraging."

"I mean, is she happy *here*, with you and me?"

"That's a funny question, Lisa." He reflected. "Ted's leaving soon. She doesn't want to give you up."

"I'm not going anyplace, not for *years*." She shook her head. "Please, Dad. Tell her—tell her not to be afraid."

"Her fears aren't altogether groundless."

Lisa shrugged. "I spend the night with friends sometimes. When we go out, a lot of them don't even tell their parents where we're going."

In his cheek, a muscle twitched. "Try to spare your mother's feelings. You know she's a worrier."

Lisa frowned. "Okay, I'll try."

"Lisa, there are things we want to know. Do you go to Aaron's house?"

"I've never been to Aaron's house. What if I had? I told you. All we do is walk and talk." Trying to control her voice, she said, "Look, Dad, Aaron is a *friend* of

97

mine. To think of him as *threatening* is just plain *sick*." Her voice went up. "Fathers are hung up on *sex*. Where their—"

He cut in. "Lisa, stop it. Don't go on. Try to think of how *we* feel."

Not giving ground, she said, "I know *exactly* how you feel."

"We love you, Lisa."

"If you really love me, Dad, give me freedom. I mean, *trust* me."

"We do, but we need reassurance sometimes. We all live together, Lisa."

"Yes, that's right. Excepting Ted. When Gina spends a weekend with her family, he stays here."

"What's Ted got to do with this?"

"Nothing. Thanks for coming up."

Her father scanned the little room, stared into the corner where she'd hung the photograph of the victims of the first atomic bombing. He turned to Lisa, touched her wrist. "Good night," he said. He kissed her cheek.

4

Shortly after one o'clock, Lisa left school, carrying her red backpack. She glanced toward Central Park, turned and walked east, heading for the subway station. A friend of hers, Naomi Kline, dark-eyed and beautiful, caught up with her. "Hello, Lisa."

"Hi, Naomi."

"Whatcha doin'?"

"Goin' home."

"There's a good show at the Whitney."

"I'm not up for a museum."

"You depressed?"

Lisa nodded. "I'm not up for anything."

"So talk to me. Let's stop at a coffee shop."

Lisa glanced at her and said, "Thanks, Naomi. Not today. There's nothing wrong. It's just that weekends are a drag. I'm bored with family gatherings."

"You're not telling me the reason you're depressed."

"I don't tell you *everything*."

Naomi nodded. "You think you got troubles, Lisa? Take my parents. They're the pits."

"That's not true. I know it's not. I've met them both."

Ignoring Lisa, she went on. "They keep me in a cocoon. I'll *never* reach the adult stage."

"What else is new?"

"It can't be as bad for you."

"I'll bet it's *worse*. Anyway, at least I'm not alone."

They parted at a DONT WALK sign. Lisa crossed Park Avenue and, in the middle of the next block, saw Aaron sitting on a step. He was wearing a goose-down jacket, jeans, and Nike running shoes. "Hi, Lisa. What—"

"Please don't say I look depressed."

"Who me? I'd never say a thing like that." As they began to walk, he said, "Your parents gave you hell last night."

"No, not really. Wish they had. I gave *them* hell. It's —I'm tired of being *protected*."

99

Aaron grinned. "This week I did a job for Uncle Bob. He paid me well. Let's have lunch in Chinatown and go to South Street afterward."

"Okay. Why not? You have to let me pay my way."

"No. Not today. You can pay for lunch next time."

"Promise? Aaron, this will be a first. We've never lunched."

"We're entering our winter phase." While they waited for a downtown local, Aaron said, "Last week a woman who had just come up from Puerto Rico chased a mugger out of here and caught his shirttail in the street. She made him drop her pocketbook."

"If you ever meet my parents, don't mention subway crime."

"Okay, I won't. Anyway, the moral of the story is, when you decide to mug someone, make sure you tuck your shirttail in."

Lisa laughed. "I'll remember."

On Canal Street, skirting a construction site, they moved uphill, toward Chinatown. Passing windows filled with jewelry, they approached a bright display of paper goods around a painted lion's head. Softly, just for Lisa's ears, Aaron strung together singsong sounds. Pushing out his upper lip, he imitated Charlie Chan.

Lisa laughed. "Aaron, stop it."

Aaron turned, as if in total innocence, frowned, pointed sadly to his chest, and made another foolish sound.

Lisa smiled. "Knock it off."

Mott Street was like a carnival, alive with people, its shopwindows filled with food: glazed fowl, candied fruit, exotic vegetables, and fish. Banners hung from restaurants. Lisa paused to look at a display of dolls and Aaron asked her, "Are you hungry?"

"Yes, I am. I'm ravenous."

"That's a 1920s word."

"How do you know?"

"I'm a literary type."

"You mean you read?"

"Only 1920s books." He took her to a narrow street and led her down a flight of stairs. "It's a kind of cave," he said.

5

The place was lit by hanging bulbs in ornate shades. The tables had Formica tops. The waiter was extremely brusque but Aaron didn't seem to mind. Aaron turned and spoke to Lisa: "Would it be presumptuous if I suggested something for you?"

She laughed. "No. Go ahead."

"Do you like squid?"

"Never had it."

"I want squid. You can try some, if you like. I'll order something else for you."

"Sure. Surprise me. You can order in Chinese."

Unruffled, Aaron ordered a squid dish and chicken with Chinese mushrooms. Lisa said, "I didn't think Jewish people ate seafood."

"Shellfish, my friend. Anyway, my family isn't Ortho-dox. They served shrimp at my bar mitzvah."

"Gosh. I wish I'd been there, Aaron."

"You must like shrimp."

Defensively, she said, "I mean, I wish I'd heard you speak."

"I wish you had." He rubbed his chin. "Lisa?"

"Yes."

"What's on your mind?"

The waiter brought a pot of tea and two small cups. Lisa poured. "I don't know why I never told my parents we were—"

"Dating."

Her eyes widened. "I suppose we *have* had dates. At first, we only met— You know. We met by accident."

"That's what you think."

Lisa blushed. "Okay, Aaron. Anyway—" She sipped her tea. "Did you tell *your* parents, Aaron?"

Aaron shrugged. "They didn't ask."

"Boys aren't *watched* the way girls are. Last night, my mother asked me where I'd been. I stalled. When Dad came home, we had our dinner right away. Mom must have talked to him as soon as I went to my room. Later on, he came upstairs. He gave me the third degree." As if confused, she let at least a minute pass before she said, "Ever since I talked to him, I've been upset. You and I—I mean, our friendship belonged to us and now it's— You know."

"Now it's common property."

"That's right. It is."

The waiter left the food and Aaron asked him for

chopsticks. The waiter shrugged, as if he didn't compre-
hend or didn't care. Making motions with his fingers,
Aaron said, "We want chopsticks!"

At last the waiter brought chopsticks, and when he'd
gone, Lisa said, "I hope you really understand—about
the way I feel, I mean." She picked up a Chinese mush-
room. It was oily, golden brown. "Hey, I like these."

"Here. Try some squid."

"Mom thinks I'm weird. I have a picture on my wall of
residents of Hiroshima, after the atomic bombing. I
insisted it be there. I mean, it's not too prominent. I'm
not morbid, honestly." She paused. "It freaked Mom out.
It made her think I needed a psychiatrist."

Aaron joked. "She may be right. I hope you're not like
my kid sister. She's a perfect Jewish princess."

"You mean spoiled?"

"Something like that."

Lisa laughed and changed the subject. "When did
you move from Borough Park to Brooklyn Heights?"

"When I was eight. My father made it really big about
that time. That was when he bought the house."

"Is it close to where we walked?"

"We walked right by the back of it."

"How come you didn't point it out?"

"I kept expecting Mom to see us. I was kind of sneak-
ing by." Lisa eyed him, and apparently to keep her quiet,
he spoke fast. "Mom said that, if we had to move, why
not buy a big apartment, maybe on Park Avenue, but
Dad just laughed and said, 'Rebecca, I'm a Brooklyn
boy.' "

"Your dad sounds great."

Aaron nodded. "He's okay. Mom's a little difficult."

"My mom's *really* difficult. She's *enormously* uptight." She paused. "We're lucky, though. We both come from happy families." Lisa dug her chopsticks underneath a wad of rice. "Hey, look," she said. "I'm learning how to use these things."

"Your father must have made it, too, to buy a house on West Tenth Street."

"Mom's grandmother grew up there, back in the nineteenth century. When she married, she moved upstate with her husband but the house stayed in the family."

"Lucky family." Aaron grinned. "How's the chicken?"

"It's delicious." Lisa took a mouthful, and before she finished chewing, she said, "Aaron?"

"Yes."

"When I talked to Mom this morning, she invited you to supper."

"Good. I'll go. Let's not keep her in suspense."

"My brother, Ted, and his friend Gina will be coming."

"Fine. I'll meet them all at once."

"I'll call Mom."

At four o'clock, they sat together on a Fulton Street doorstep, looking out across the polished cobblestones, resting up from touring South Street, and the maritime museum. Having had enough of ships and river smells, Lisa said, "C'mon. Let's go."

"Homesick?"

"No." She laughed. "We can't go to my house yet. I mean we can but—"

"We can hang out in the Square."

"And check out shops along Eighth Street."

As they stood up, Aaron asked, "You want to walk?"
"No, I'd rather take the subway."

6

In the subway Aaron said, "This time of day, the last car's best."

She nodded. "Right." A train came in and Lisa, moving with the throng, stepped aboard, Aaron following behind. As the doors began to close, they nudged his shoulders, then slid back to let him in. At last, like toothless gums, they shut. The train began to move again.

Lisa and Aaron found a seat. As they sat down, Lisa put her backpack on her knees, and right away, across the car, she saw a boy about sixteen watching her. He was pale and had dark hair. He stared fixedly at her through a pair of tinted glasses. There was something in his look that made her take a fast, involuntary breath. He was with a smaller boy, tense and wiry, highly charged.

The train slowed down, and as it stopped, Lisa almost cautioned Aaron, telling him to be on guard, but decided she might be creating problems if she did. The train began to roll again.

As if to tell his friend to watch, the boy who wore the tinted glasses glanced at Lisa. As he made his move, she whispered, "Here comes trouble."

"So I see." Aaron stood up.

"Careful, Aaron." Lisa, clutching at her backpack, got up, too.

The boy's eyes narrowed. "Givin' me your seat?" he asked.

As Lisa spoke, her lips grew pale. "If you want it."

Aaron said, "Look, why don't you—"

The boy pushed Aaron. "You sit down!"

Aaron staggered and recovered. Standing straight, touching Lisa's arm, he spoke. His voice was shaking. "Let's go, Lisa. Our stop's next."

The boy took Lisa by the wrist. "Before you go, I'd like a souvenir," he said.

"Let go of me!" She twisted loose.

Aaron moved in. His voice cracked but he was firm. "Don't you touch my friend again."

The boy faced Aaron, giving him a chilly look. "You're in trouble."

Lisa's heart was racing, pounding. "Go away!"

The boy's face reddened and a woman sitting near them said, "You kids fight some other place."

The boy said, "Lady, shut your mouth."

As she got up to move away, the woman said, "I'm gonna call a Transit cop."

The boy gave her a vicious shove. She fell backward and collapsed against the seat. She drew a breath and started screaming. Aaron stepped between the woman and the boy, but even so, the woman gasped and screamed again. Another woman, near the door, began to yell. Aaron, talking to the boy, said, "Look, before the cops come, why don't you get off the train?"

The train stopped. In a wild, frenetic motion, saving face, the boy reached out and, snatching Lisa's backpack, spun away and bolted toward an exit, followed by the other boy. Aaron, pushing past a clot of passengers,

dashed after them. Lisa followed. The first boy cata-
pulted toward the stairs and the other, blocked by people
coming through the turnstiles, paused just long enough
so Aaron could catch up with him. The boy half turned,
to fend him off, and Aaron caught him by his jacket and
pushed him against a wall. The boy bounced back. As he
moved, Lisa saw a bright, metallic flash between them
and she screamed, "He has a knife!" She froze. Trapped,
the boy glanced toward the nearest turnstile. Aaron
grabbed the boy's knife arm and wrenched it, forcing
him to drop the weapon.

Trembling, Lisa stared down at the knife. With her
foot, she pushed it clear. She saw the boy break Aaron's
grip, push through a gate, and disappear. When Aaron
made no move to follow, she looked closely. Blood was
running down his hand.

Other people who had left the train had walked
around them, skirting what had seemed to them a dan-
gerous scuffle. Several stragglers were still moving toward
the exits and an older couple, entering, pushed through
a turnstile close to them.

Lisa rolled up Aaron's sleeve and saw the cut. "Hold
your arm up." Reaching into her hip pocket, she pulled
out a bright red cotton bandanna and wrapped his wrist.
The older man, who had just come through the turnstile,
asked what he could do for them. "My friend's been
hurt." The man was kind and Lisa almost asked him to
go with them to the street, but she said, "We'll be okay.
I'll take him to the hospital."

As they passed the token booth, the man on duty
beckoned to them. Speaking through his microphone, he
said, "I called the police."

On the sidewalk Lisa said, "No sign of them. Are you bleeding very much?"

"Your bandanna is soaked through."

Lisa scanned the intersection. "No cabs in sight. We'd better—"

"There's a police car."

Lisa stepped into the street and flagged the car. As it pulled up to the curb, the driver, spoke to them, without compassion. "What's the trouble?"

Aaron said, "My friend was mugged and I was cut."

The driver's partner, who had soft, Hispanic eyes, ducked out and stood beside the car. "Here. Get in. We'll take you to a hospital."

Lisa asked, "Can you take us to St. Vincent's? It's two blocks from where I live."

The dark-eyed man said, "We can do that, can't we, Pat?"

As the car began to move, Pat turned the siren on. When they approached Fifth Avenue and slowed down for a traffic jam, the driver said, "We'll be filing a report. My partner, here, will write it up."

His partner said, "I'm Officer Rodriguez."

The police car parked on Seventh Avenue, behind an ambulance disgorging several paramedics and a patient on a stretcher. Officer Rodriguez said, "I'll take him in."

Lisa told him, "I'll go, too."

He shook his head. "Better go around the corner. There's a waiting room in there."

Lisa did as she was told. She sat down on a wooden bench. It wasn't long before Rodriguez came and sat next to her. "He's okay. He won't have to be admitted." As he made out his report, he asked her what had been in her backpack. Lisa said, "Not much. An English book, a pad, and maybe three Bic pens. My money is in my pocket." She stared down at her hands and saw that they were shaking. "Look at that."

Rodriguez nodded. "Lots of people get that way after something violent happens."

Aaron came out, with a bandage on his wrist, grinned, and said, "I'm gonna live."

Rodriguez asked him for his street address and had him look at his report. Then he said goodbye and left. Aaron glanced at his watch. "It's five-thirty. What time did your mother want us?"

"I said we'd be there at six."

"Okay. Let's find a place where we can wait."

Sitting in a small restaurant, tracing patterns on a wooden tabletop, Lisa didn't say a word. Aaron asked her, "Are you worried?"

Lisa shrugged. "I just need to settle down. I'm glad we have a little time before we have to face my mom."

The waitress brought two cups of herbal tea. As Lisa sipped, Aaron said, "You make your mother sound like a Dahoman warrior."

Lisa said reflectively, "She's not that bad. It's just—" She grit her teeth. "When she hears about this little episode, she'll flip."

7

At ten minutes after six, they turned into Lisa's block. As they approached her doorstep, Lisa said, "Last night, when I came home, I knew I'd have to tell the truth about the reason I was late." She climbed the steps. "I was sorry. Now I'm glad."

"Are you sure you don't wish things had stayed the same?"

"Things don't ever stay the same." She laughed. "For example, I'm at least two inches taller than I was at Christmastime." As she unlocked the door, she asked, "In December, do you have a Christmas tree?"

"No, we don't."

"You can come and see our tree. In fact, I'll put a present under it, for you know who." As they stepped inside the house, Lisa shouted, "Hello, Mom!"

"I'll be with you in a second. Let me put the chicken in." They heard the oven door slam shut and Lisa's mother came right out. She said, "Aaron, good to meet you."

Aaron was a little shy. "Thanks for asking me to supper."

"Glad to have you. Lisa, show him where we hang our coats." Looking back at him, she asked, "Whatever happened to your wrist?"

Quickly Lisa said, "We were mugged this afternoon, in the subway. One kid flashed a knife at us and Aaron took the knife away."

Lisa's mother stared at them. Her eyes grew large. "What made them pick on *you*?"

Lisa said, "Slow down, Mom. You talk as if—"

"Don't be so defensive, Lisa. I just want to find out what—"

"You just want to bore in deeper. Look. We were

scared." She paused. Her voice grew husky as she said, "We've just come home. Can't you see—"

"Why are you so secretive?"

Working to control herself, Lisa spoke, "I was secretive last night. Tonight I'm not. You haven't given me a chance to tell you *anything*. The boy who brought the whole thing on was psychopathic. He was borderline at best. He stared at me at least five minutes, then he started bugging us."

"When you saw that he was staring, shouldn't you have turned away?"

Lisa's lips were white as chalk. "You weren't *there*." Her voice went up. "You're making tons of suppositions, based on *total* ignorance."

Aaron looked down at his bandage, touched it, spoke. "Mrs. Mackintosh, I—"

Interrupting, Lisa's mother asked him, "Would you like to call your parents?"

"No. No, thanks. They know I'm here. No matter what I said to them, they'd send an ambulance for me."

Lisa's mother's manner changed. "This is not a joking matter."

Lisa's voice broke. "Aaron has a right to joke and so have I. If you'd been through a thing like this, you'd come home and have a drink, a good *stiff* drink. Joking is a way of—" Lisa's face was streaked with tears. Smearing them, she turned to Aaron. "Let's go to the TV room."

Lisa's mother said, "No, wait. Let's talk."

Lisa swung away from her. "Later, maybe. When you want to be polite."

Stricken, Lisa's mother said, "Please. Let's talk now."

"*No. Not now.* I need some space."

As they went up, Lisa heard a shower running on the third floor. She said, "Ted is home."

The TV room was littered with back copies of *The New York Times* and *TV Guide*. A couch and two chairs faced a color television set. She turned on a standing lamp. "Now you've met her. Now you see. She's not always rational."

Aaron sat down on the couch. He coughed. "Who is?"

"No need to be so tolerant. Can't you see—"

Aaron whispered, "You're right. Your mother wasn't rational."

"Sorry, Aaron. I'm on edge."

He was silent for a while. "There's a reason I'm so tolerant of mothers, ones who *try*. After all, your mother's trying. I—"

"Go on."

"*My* mother's not just difficult. She's— Promise you won't talk about it?"

Lisa frowned. "Sure, I promise."

"We'd only been in Brooklyn Heights about a week when Mom broke down. She spent six weeks away from home, in a private institution."

Lisa whispered, "Gosh. I'm sorry."

"People who are insecure hate making moves. You know, they hate to see things change. Mom talked about Park Avenue but she clung to Borough Park, to our tiny, crummy house. Brooklyn Heights is beautiful—" He closed his eyes.

"I understand."

"I hope you *never* understand. It's frightening to see a lost and hunted look on the face of someone you—"

In a small voice, Lisa asked, "Is she okay?"

"Sure. She's okay." He shrugged. "We worry, though. We always will."

Lisa said reflectively, "When Mom was just about my age, her father died. He was killed in World War II. She mentions him from time to time but—"

"Gosh, that's sad. Why don't you remember that, instead of thinking of the Hiroshima victims?" Quickly, softly, Aaron added, "I'm just echoing my dad. One night, two years or so ago, I invoked the Holocaust, to try to make my mother's pain seem trivial. I've never seen Dad angrier. I can't repeat the things he said."

Lisa looked down at her hands. She stood up. "I'll be right back." Going upstairs to her room, she took down the photograph of the Hiroshima victims, rolled it up, and put it on her closet shelf. Back in the hall, she heard her brother in the bathroom, singing softly to himself. She said, "Ted?"

Ted's head appeared. He had a handsome, slightly humorous face and bright blue eyes. "Hello, Lisa."

"Hi. Where's Gina? I thought she was coming, too."

"She'll be here soon."

"Good. I like her." Lowering her voice, she added, "Please don't dress up much tonight. I brought a friend. He didn't have a chance to change."

"What's he wearing?"

"Jeans, a shirt, and running shoes."

"No socks?"

"Black socks."

"I'll wear something similar."

"Sometimes I conquer my dislike of you, for fifteen minutes at a time."

"This is worth at least an hour."

"Maybe so. Another thing. He has a bandage on his wrist. Let Mom or Dad be the first to mention it. If you fail to notice it, I'll be good as gold all weekend. If you're lucky, I might take you to the zoo."

Back in the TV room, Lisa said, "I took down the photograph."

"What photo— Oh, the one of the Hiroshima victims. Good. I'm glad."

Lisa heard her mother in the front hall greeting Gina. "Hey, there's Gina. Let's go down."

8

During what her parents called the cocktail hour, Lisa's father mixed the drinks. Her mother cooked. Lisa, who wanted to avoid the kitchen for a while, set the table.

As she sat down with the others, Lisa took a sip of V-8 juice and bit into her lemon peel. She was watchful, not engaging in small talk. Ted and Aaron found a patch of common ground. They discussed the city's landmarks and its history. Her father, who liked Gina very much and was telling her a story, glanced at Aaron once too often and gave Lisa sidelong looks. Lisa knew her mother had been talking to her father and had told him what had happened. She only wished he'd mention it and clear the air.

114

As they sat down at the table, Lisa's father said, to no one in particular, "I'd like to bless the food tonight." Knowing Ted was an agnostic, he winked at his son and said, "Give me leave to speak to God."

Ted smiled. "This is a free country, Dad."

Lisa's father turned to Aaron. "Aaron, do you bless your food?"

Aaron said, "On Friday nights, my father reads from Genesis. We bless the wine."

Lisa's father bowed his head. "Bless, O Lord, this food to our use and us to Thy service." He turned to Aaron. "Thanks for coming. I mean on your holy day. I hope your parents weren't distressed—"

Lisa rapped the table hard. "That's enough about religion!" She went on. "This afternoon we went to lunch in Chinatown. After that, we went to South Street, to the maritime museum. Coming here, we took a subway. We were mugged."

Ted let out a long, low whistle.

Lisa's father poked the chicken with a fork. "Aaron, tell us how it started."

Aaron told them what had happened. When he'd finished, Gina said, "We do everything we can to avoid that kind of thing. We ride the middle cars at night, because more people sit in them. We're alert, but those things are bound to happen."

Lisa's mother spoke to Aaron. "You were brave."

"I just did what seemed necessary."

Quietly, but with great determination, Lisa's mother said, "There are many kinds of courage." Sensing her intensity, the others waited as she stared down at her plate. Taking a deep breath, she said, "My father fought in World War II. He gave his life for all of us." She bit her lip. "The day we learned—"

Lisa whispered, "Go on, Mom."

Lisa's mother told the story of the day she'd heard about her father's death. Her voice was strong until she said, "That night, a boy named Gary Mackintosh was brave enough—"

Gently coming to her rescue, Lisa's father said, "I took her walking on the beach. Now, looking back, we know we fell in love that night."

9

Gina left after supper. Later, in the living room, Lisa's mother spoke to Aaron. "Please forgive me for being upset when I heard about what happened on the subway."

"That's okay. My mother would have been the same." He blushed. "I mean, most mothers, hearing that their daughter had been through a thing like that, would be in a state of shock."

"I'm glad you were with her, Aaron." With an almost wistful look, she added, "I know I'm an anxious mother. I come by it naturally. My mother was an anxious person."

Ted carried out the coffee cups and helped his mother clear the table. As they finished and came back, Aaron stood up. "Guess it's time for me to go."

Lisa said, "I'll walk a block or two with you."

"If it's okay with your parents."

Lisa's father, looking more concerned for Aaron than for his daughter, told him, "Let me give you cab fare, please."

"Thank you, Mr. Mackintosh. It's only ten. The trains are full this time of night. I'll be okay."

"Be sure to ride the middle car." He winked, and said, "Unless they come in even numbers."

They left the house. The street was quiet. Only distant, muffled sounds came from the busy avenues. Overhead, the sky was clear. Lisa spotted several stars. A ship's horn sounded on the Hudson. Aaron spoke. "Lisa?"

"Yes."

"I think your mother's wonderful."

"Mom has her points."

"I'll say she has."

"It seems unfair that now you have to go back home and face it all a second time."

Clowning, joking, Aaron said, "This is what I face tonight." He struck his forehead with his fist as his mother might have done. "I told your father long ago, 'I don't want my son to die. Subways are beyond the question. Who can trust a taxi driver? We got money. Hire the boy a limousine.'"

"You're as mean as I am, Aaron. Is your father anxious, too?"

"If I tell you everything, you'll never want to visit us."

When they reached Fifth Avenue, Aaron said, "Tonight I want to play it safe. I'll watch you walk along Tenth Street and climb your steps. I'll stay right here until you're inside your house."

"Okay, Aaron."

"Good night, Lisa."

SEA CHANGE

As Lisa entered the front hall, she heard her mother and her brother in the kitchen. Her father, coming down the stairs, said, "I liked Aaron very much."

"I knew you would." Lisa went up to her room. When she'd put her nightgown on and brushed her teeth, she went downstairs. Passing through the living room, she saw her father dozing. In the kitchen, Ted smiled. "Hey there, Sis."

"If you call me Sis again, I won't take you to the zoo."

Her mother looked at her and smiled. "I'll come and tuck you in tonight."

As Lisa moved back through the living room, her father stirred and she bent down and kissed his head. He smiled that special smile of his and said, "Good night."

Lisa, lying in her bed and waiting, fell asleep. When she woke up, she found her mother sitting by her, eyes wide open, motionless. Lisa saw a glint of gold below her throat. In a small and sleepy voice, she said, "Your locket. You don't wear it very often."

"It belonged to your grandmother."

Lisa sat up. "Yes, I know. You told me all about it once."

"So I did." Her mother glanced across the room. Seeming puzzled, she said, "Lisa?"

Lisa nodded. "I took down the photograph of the victims of the first atomic bombing."

"Why?"

"It was something Aaron said—"

"You don't have to tell me now."

"Okay, I won't."

"Some other time."

"I love you, Mom."

7